Acidic Fiction

Acidic Fiction #1

Corrosive Chronicles

Edited by Steven x Davis

The stories in this book were originally published between
July 1, 2014 and December 31, 2014 on www.acidicfiction.com.

ISBN-10: 0-692-40347-7
ISBN-13: 978-0-692-40347-1

We have it in our power to begin the world over again.

– Thomas Paine

Table of Contents

Foreword
Starting from Square One

I started *Acidic Fiction* in 2014 because I was frustrated with the content and submission processes of online speculative fiction magazines. Most of the stories I read in mainstream or well-regarded sci-fi/fantasy magazines took place in alternate universes that were profoundly different from the real world.

Science fiction and fantasy authors love to create new universes out of whole cloth, but that means a large portion of each story must be dedicated to detailed descriptions of the setting, often lengthening the story considerably and delaying or interrupting the narrative. In short stories and flash fiction, where space is at a premium, this level of exposition often comes at the expense of every other story element.

It also seems that magazines place a great deal of importance on credentials and established names at the expense of finding exceptional stories by new authors. When they do look for new authors, most speculative fiction magazines cast an extremely wide net, accepting as many submissions as possible with very few restrictions on subject matter or content.

Naturally, these magazines receive tons of submissions from a huge variety of authors, yet they usually respond to those authors with form rejections or an implied rejection in the form of silence. In my opinion, this submission process is highly inefficient and frustrating for authors and editors alike.

So I decided to start my own magazine. I wanted to avoid these problems, so I made a few choices at the outset:

First, the magazine would publish stories that take place in a contemporary setting. By publishing stories set in a world that is only slightly different from reality, I can look for stories that focus on all aspects of storytelling instead of just the setting. I called it "contemporary speculative fiction" so people would have an idea of what to expect. It also happens to be the genre I enjoy reading (and writing) the most.

Second, the submission process would not require authors to submit any information about themselves, their credentials, or their previous published works. My goal is always to find the best possible stories, so I read all submissions blind. I base my decisions completely on the stories themselves, not their authors.

Third, I would respond personally to story submissions. Any stories that don't meet the submission requirements get a form rejection, but all other stories receive at least a few quick notes on their content and execution. If the only problem with a submission is that the story doesn't fit the tone of the magazine or my personal taste, I offer some encouragement so authors know they're on the right track.

I don't view these personal rejections as a waste of effort, however, because they help authors improve their writing. If the authors don't know what's wrong with their submissions, they're likely to submit similar stories with similar problems in the future, so I can save myself some future effort by addressing those problems early on.

Furthermore, if the authors can fix the problems with their stories, it will prevent editors from other magazines from having to read the same story with the same flaws, thus (hopefully) benefitting authors and editors the world over.

Finally, I would pay authors a flat rate per story. The decision to pay the authors was a no-brainer, largely because I understood the difficulty of getting paid for my own writing. I also knew that payments, even small ones, would attract more writers and better stories.

The decision to pay per story was based on the fact that in my experience, the quality of a story has nothing to do with its length. Payment by the word also seems archaic for online magazines, where there is no practical difference between transmitting ten words or 10,000. Therefore, stories on the site can be as long or as short as necessary without affecting the payment. It also makes my bookkeeping much simpler.

Time will tell if this publishing philosophy is viable, but the first six months were very successful.

I began the process of starting the magazine in July 2014. I chose the name *Acidic Fiction* because I liked the assonance of the phrase, the dark tone it conveyed, and the potential for "acidic" visual designs. The name was also completely available online and not trademarked.

I bought the domain name and email addresses in early July, then registered accounts on Twitter, Facebook, and Reddit. On July 30, 2014, I organized *Acidic Fiction* as a limited-liability corporation in the State of Kansas.

In early August, I set up the website framework using my haphazard knowledge of WordPress and CSS. My brother designed the logos, icons, banners, backgrounds, and color scheme in exchange for a Super Nintendo game cartridge (without getting too specific, it involves time-traveling adolescent reptiles). I was so dedicated to making sure the stories on the site were properly edited that I even purchased my own hardcover copy of *The Chicago Manual of Style*.

At the end of August, I began accepting story submissions. I started purchasing stories in early September and published the first story ("Lester and The Doctor") on September 22, 2014.

I had no idea what to expect when I started reading submissions, whether I'd get too many or too few, whether they'd be too short or too long, whether they'd be flawless or unreadable, or whether they would even fit the submission guidelines.

When I finally did go through the submissions to the site, I found a mixture of everything, good and bad, along with several surprises. I tended to accept stories that surprised me in a good way, and I'd say the overall process of reading and accepting stories has been a pleasant surprise.

By the end of 2014, I had published 32 short stories on the site. From those, I selected 14 exceptional stories to anthologize in this book, showcasing a wide variety of genres, settings, characters, and voices. I was truly lucky to receive so many awesome stories last year ... if you believe in luck, of course.

Hopefully this will be the first of many *Acidic Fiction* anthologies to come. In the meantime, enjoy the excellent stories in this book and the new stories published on the site every week.

Thank you very much for reading.

Steven x Davis
Editor-in-chief, *Acidic Fiction*

Lester and The Doctor
by H. C. Duncan

A disheveled, glassy-eyed man with a nine o'clock shadow enters a dimly lit office above a bank. Unlike the linoleum in the sterile reception area, the carpet is new, and he feels the urge to take his shoes off, to feel the wool, soft and lovely under his toes.

The Doctor, who isn't wearing a white coat or stethoscope but is still a doctor, asks him with a pleasant smile to sit down. There are plaques behind The Doctor's desk—not as many as Lester has seen in other offices, but enough to convey a sense of respectability.

Lester doesn't know how he should sit. Maybe lying down will present itself as an option soon; it seems more natural in a situation like this. Maybe he'll take his shoes off when he lies down so he can feel the carpet.

Lester takes a gamble and sits normally, maybe slumping a little too much, but The Doctor doesn't do anything strange. He clicks a pen and goes to write Lester's name, realizes he just unclicked the pen, clicks it again, writes with a flourish, looks up with a smack of his lips and says, "So!"

Lester wants to cry. The whole thing feels too real. Never in a million years did he think he'd be seeing a psychiatrist.

"When did the nightmares begin, Mr. Hill?" The Doctor asks.

Lester is chilly, but Doctor seems warm in his big leather chair. A patch of enticing sunlight is slowly sliding its way up the couch like a nervous teenager's hand, but until it reaches him, he will have to suffer in air-conditioned discomfort.

"About a week ago."

1

"So, September 6th?" The Doctor prompts.

"Right."

"Tell me about them." The Doctor looks down and flips through several sheets of paper.

All Lester gave the receptionist was his name, address, and an insurance card. Why does The Doctor need a clipboard? Is his whole history going to come out here? Hopefully not.

"All I want is some sleeping pills," Lester says, one arm scratching the other.

"And I understand you went to your regular doctor to get some. Because of your behavior there, Dr. Townley asked me to take a look at you first."

The Doctor smiles politely and looks up, like an inattentive father glancing over his newspaper after admonishing his five-year-old son. He has a perfectly sculpted white beard that makes him look like Colonel Sanders, or an insane chicken farmer, or both, someone who seems nice and friendly, but also the kind of psycho that experiments on his dead—

"Mr. Hill, I understand you've been suffering from insomnia, correct?"

"It's not insomnia," Lester replies, "I just don't want to go to sleep."

"You refuse to go to sleep without sleeping pills, then, or some form of sleeping aid."

"Call it what you like."

"And you've been having nightmares. That's the crux of what I want to discuss."

"I have. And you're going to try and determine what's causing the dreams, I guess?"

"I'm just going to have a look at the whole of you to see what the matter is." The Doctor paused. "Dr. Townley said that you mentioned some issues with your wife, as well."

Lester and The Doctor

"He did? No, no, no. This has nothing to do with that." Lester runs a hand through his sweaty hair before going on. "Sorry, I've never done anything like this before." He hesitates, concentrates, and continues.

"A week ago, these dreams started. They were just regular nightmares at first. The first two nights, I'd be having a regular, you know, normal dream, holding hands with a girl, picnicking in the garden, whatever. Then something would change, and I'd be staring at a black hole, the middle of nothing, and there'd be a scream, and I'd wake up, drenched in sweat. It's basically ruined my sheets."

The Doctor waits for his patient to continue. Lester begins to notice the air-conditioner running in the room, its hum like something mechanical clearing its throat.

"But then, on the third night—this is September 8th—it seems like I went straight from regular nighttime thoughts to the black hole dream."

"A black hole, you're calling it?"

"Yeah. I've had recurring nightmares before, right? We all have. I used to have a clown nightmare that got me five days in a row."

"Sure."

"But this is different. It's like I have no choice; it just starts playing the second I close my eyes. I hear my wife call my name—this isn't always the setup, just an example—I hear her call me, 'Lester,' then I turn around, and there's a black hole where her face should be. It's like the dream sets me up, it makes me happy, puts me in this happy place, and then it automatically ruins it.

"The black hole is a huge, colossal spiral that's just twisting and sucking in air, with little blinking lights surrounding it, contorting everything. And it isn't just contained to her face; it drips down to her chest. It's like this living thing that eroded her whole head and it's trying to suck me in with it."

The Doctor nods silently, drawing a small black circle on

his paper.

"So when did you start staying up all night? Was that to combat the dreams?" The Doctor's voice is hoarse, like he's been shouting loudly into a pillow.

"Three days ago, when I saw Dr. Townley. That was the first night I didn't sleep."

"Perhaps your sleeplessness contributed to your irritability," The Doctor says without looking up.

Lester sighs and looks out the window to the beach. "Every time I try to sleep, the nightmares start. I think the lack of sleep is making me delusional. I've started seeing things, even when I'm awake. That's why I'm here."

The Doctor's hand stops spiraling, hesitates, and continues, the pen easily pressing an indentation through several sheets of paper.

"What kinds of things?" The Doctor asks, his voice catching in his throat.

The hum of the air-conditioner is louder. It's no longer an undercurrent of the conversation; Lester feels he actually has to actively speak over it. He doesn't speak of it, though. Drawing attention to the noise would look paranoid.

"I work at a cafe near the beach—"

"Which one?"

He points to the window. "That one. Beachview."

The circle is larger now, the outline of a new shape encompassing the first one, black ink filling in the gaps.

"I've been there." The Doctor clears his throat again. "Good, uh, coffee."

"I do regular dishwashing stuff, serving customers, you know, the usual. The other day, we were closing up early, around three. Business hasn't been so great lately."

The Doctor's heart rate is rising, and beads of sweat are starting to appear in his hairline, the air conditioner hums onward endlessly, He tries to mouth, "Of course."

"I was taking a breather, standing on the footpath outside. I was tired and my eyes were stinging, so I wasn't really paying attention to the world, but I saw something on the beach that didn't look right to me."

The Doctor widens the path of the circle, starts holding onto the pen so tight the plastic gives way a little, bending in his hand.

"There was this woman out in the surf, standing still. If I hadn't been watching her, I wouldn't have noticed that she wasn't moving. Does that makes sense?"

The Doctor gives a noncommittal grunt, his voice a little higher than natural, and Lester continues.

"The woman was just standing there with her back to the sea. She's wearing a real big dress, black and lacy, like a wedding dress or something. And I'm standing there watching her, wondering what the deal is, and slowly, she starts moving towards land."

He looks up to see if The Doctor wants him to keep going. Lester has chills running through his body, remembering the woman and the way her face looked, the black lipstick and dead eyes.

The Doctor isn't even looking at him; instead, he's ferociously writing something in his little notepad, his breath audible. Annoyed, Lester continues.

"It's like the other people on the beach can't even see her. They get out of her way to allow for some room around her, but it's unintentional. She's wading toward the shore, and I don't know how she's moving through the waves. I couldn't work it out, but they weren't blocking her path at all."

Lester thinks that maybe The Doctor is engaging in some sort of radical psychiatric treatment where he ignores the patient, who's lying there, incredibly fragile, getting him to open up out of spite. He pushes on through the discomfort and the annoyance, through the sound of the machine humming and groaning.

"And I mean, this isn't a dream, I'm watching this happen right in front of me, maybe 50 feet away. There are cars going by, people walking past, and people in the water with her. Do you know what I mean?"

The Doctor doesn't answer. He's stuck, his neck stiff and vibrating slightly, his eyes wide and starting to tear up, glistening in the low and dusty light.

"Do you? I mean, I understand that the dreams are just something in my subconscious, but if I'm starting to hallucinate, I'm in serious trouble. And if it wasn't a hallucination …"

The Doctor's eyelids start to tremble and the pen snaps. He goes on drawing with the nub of it, thick black circles around and around, harder and harder. The scratching of the pen is audible over Lester's talking and the air conditioning, which is as loud as jet engine now. The sun hasn't moved in five minutes and the temperature is dropping considerably.

"Doctor?"

Around and around, the scratching continues.

Lester stands up, eying the silent man whose eyes won't follow him. They're stuck on his former position on the couch. Lester puts an arm on The Doctor's shoulder, shaking him lightly, trying to bring him back to reality. The air conditioner screams on full blast, sending out sheets of icy air coupled with a noise that neither of them have ever heard before.

The Doctor comes to, looks up, and screams. Lester sees the terror in his eyes, in his mouth, in the spiderweb of spit hanging between his teeth.

Instead of Lester's face, all The Doctor sees is a spiraling black galaxy of darkness, moving slowly towards him, swallowing him up.

Roll the Sky
by Yegor Chekmarev

I really wish I could remember simple things, like Daddy's face. Then I wouldn't have to hide behind the stones and statues whenever he comes by. If I knew Daddy was back to see me, I could finally hug him and tell him everything is okay.

See, there's this man walking alone down the main winding path. He's dressed in a dapper black suit with his gray hair parted. When he comes by, I hide behind an obelisk. I don't know who this man is, but I have a good feeling about him. I've had a lot of good feelings before, but this one is the strongest. I found fresh flowers on the ground earlier, and I know Daddy came by not too long ago. Who else are they for, if not for me?

Because the sun has finally come out, today is a good day. The cloudless sky is a wonderful bright blue, and my dress ripples gently in the breeze. I decide that the man is my father and that he's coming to see me again. Today is a good day and I want to be right.

But he's not carrying any flowers and he's walking too fast. He's scowling, with a set, tense jaw. Daddy wouldn't be smiling, though. It's hard to smile in a place like this, but it makes things better. Whenever I feel sadness coming, I just give myself a little shake of the head and a slight smile. It hurts for a moment, but it works. I wish he would smile.

He stops at one of the stones near the back. Maybe it's a friend's. Maybe it's mine. Where is my stone? Another simple thing I can't remember. Was there a ceremony recently? They all blend together, grimly dressed families standing around a fancy box, weeping, crying, and always softly. It's just a box. There's nothing in it.

I hate how the families look. I'm always wearing a white dress, and even though it sometimes gets dirty, it's much better than the drab, faded black that all of the other girls and women wear. The men and boys look like soldiers in their identical black suits.

They march, stone-faced, up and down the paths, and I trail behind, out of sight. One of the men stops, eyes shut as tight as a vise, but the tears still slide out. He tries to stifle himself but it sounds like he's choking. No one comes to help him, so I run over and hug him.

His memories rush into me and every single part of my body is screaming to let go because it hurts so much to remember. But I don't dare let go. We collapse to our knees and I can see and feel everything. The anger, the grief, the sheer sadness pounds at us, but I can't let go.

After a bit, the crying slows down, the breaths become deeper and less ragged, and the man stands up, wipes his eyes, and keeps walking. No more marching. No more hiding. I try to hold onto the memories like jewelry, but they're more like shards of ice. Soon, they melt and fall through my hands.

There's so much crying for the loved ones. I want to tell everyone that they aren't suffering anymore. I like to think that it was their time and they were tired. Here, they get to rest.

If one of them decides to come out and say hi to me, that would be nice too.

I creep closer. Daddy is still standing by the stone. He hasn't moved in ages. Sometimes he stares off into the distance as the occasional car flits by on Witherspoon Avenue. Sometimes he looks down at the stone and covers his mouth with his hands.

When it gets dark, Jerald closes the gates and locks them with a rusty, wheezing padlock. He spends the whole day in his office. He doesn't come out to say hi to anyone. He dreams about his wife and kids but I have never seen them visit him. When I stop by to say hi, it sometimes feels like he's actually looking at me. I think he's even smiled once or twice, but it's a sad smile that doesn't linger very long.

After Jerald goes home, I go back to my tree to sleep. It's an old sycamore off of one of the smaller paths. When I touch it, it tells me it's been here for a million years and will be right here for a million more. It's always cool and dark under the tree, and when I have trouble sleeping, I like to listen to the world slowing down. The wind stops whispering through the branches above and begins to howl. Some nights it really gets bad. I can't imagine what's scaring the poor wind. Surely it can just flow through and around everyone?

There's the crunch of leaves underneath the shoes of someone going home to their family, the click of a lamp turning off in a bedroom, the sliding of deadbolts as doors are locked until morning. And then you expect silence, but instead you can suddenly hear the ground, crawling with nasty little bugs that aren't so nasty when you don't think about them.

You can hear the heartbeat of an entire town. Do you know what the funny part is? It sounds like someone is pitter-pattering randomly on some soft drums at first, but when the sleep gets as deep as the night, then it's all one, steady pulse. All of these people, never really knowing anyone outside of their house or apartment, but at night they all breathe the same.

Sometimes when I'm lost in silly thoughts like these, I feel the ground vibrate. Cats pad around on the concrete and grass, and they even try to sneak up on me. They don't know that I heard them a mile away. Right as they prepare to pounce, I roar at them! You should see the looks on their faces! They jump nearly ten feet in the air and scamper away, scared half to death.

In the middle of the night, kids sometimes climb over the fence and do stupid kid things. I like to think I've outgrown them, but I can't even remember how old I'm supposed to be. It looks like they're having fun, even when they bring drugs, alcohol, and spray paint. They try to be quiet, but they're always giggling and shushing each other.

I've seen some of them dance on the grass, trying to be funny. They think they're dancing on other people's loved ones, but there's no one beneath them. I dance with them in the dark because it's too loud to sleep. After they get tired of dancing, they drink and smoke and paint some of the bigger stones.

When everything slows down and the kids stop dancing and get sad, that's when I go to hug them. Their memories are soft and muted, like butterfly kisses. They're happy, they're bored, and they have problems with friends and family, but they don't know what pain is. They haven't dealt with the grief that the older visitors have.

When I let go, they finally go home, tired but hopefully less confused. Jerald gets grumbly at them in the mornings, but he knows how to clean the paint off the stones. It gives him something to do. I don't get mad at all. They're just kids, they're not trying to be mean. There just isn't much to do in this town.

Daddy finally moves, dropping to his knees at the stone. He's talking to himself now, and the blue sky above him is spotless. It's a beautiful day, yet he acts so strange. The left side of his jacket hangs lower than the right, and sometimes he pats it to make sure whatever he's carrying is still there. Then, he looks around but there's no one. Jerald is having lunch right now, a peanut butter and jelly sandwich with banana slices, along with a small flask of whiskey.

Daddy's hands are restless but he doesn't caress the stone as others do with their loved ones. He stands up, reaches into his jacket, and pulls out something shiny. I can't make out what it is. He holds it high above his head and it catches the sun. A hammer!

I hold my breath as he brings it down hard on the stone. It connects like a firing pin to the back of a bullet. The crack splits the air, echoing in the stillness of the day. After it passes over, I forget to breathe. Daddy hangs his head over the stone, his right arm hanging limply at his side.

Roll the Sky

When he takes in a deep breath and raises the hammer again, I run out from behind the stone yelling "Daddy! Stop!"

He brings the hammer down with both hands. A comet's tail of dust shoots into the air, and the earth below our feet cracks in half like a fissure. My ears are ringing and it's hard to keep my balance. I keep running, yelling, "Daddy, Daddy, Daddy!"

I see him clearly as he raises it for the third time. Sweat drips from his temples, his eyes wide, white, and red, and he's so angry, terrible, and frightening. His teeth are clenched, but spit hangs on his lower lip, his neck is taut and tense with all the veins and arteries bulging out, wrapped around his throat like a noose. I'm so close to hugging him. I want to comfort him but he can't hear me at all, and when I finally touch him—

Leaves whisper on the road. The odor of gasoline cuts through the chilly breeze of the afternoon. It is cold outside, but inside the two tangled cars, it is still warm and dusty. Something is beeping and everyone is still.

The hospital is covered in a layer of gauze. The nurses are mummies. It hurts so much to move. The pills don't really help. He sits there, wishing he was dead so that he doesn't have to wait. The doctors give him the good news.

The house is empty. He is waiting by the TV day and night, always drinking coffee and always smoking cigarettes. His eyes are always closed but he can't fall asleep. The phone rings. The bad news arrives. On the TV, the news reporter flashes the faces and names, one young, one old, both beautiful. He leans back and opens his mouth to scream.

There is a third face, a third name. He waits for a long time, repeating it over and over again until it burns in his mind like a flare and he can't sleep.

His jacket is heavy. He walks right past their stones, the first two names already receding, and goes for the third name.

—I pull back and crumple to the ground. I was wrong. My daddy wouldn't have so much hate in his heart. He's scaring me and I can't help him. That scares me even more. I've given him pause with my touch, but I won't be able to wrap my arms around him and let him cry into me because he's too busy swinging the hammer. He's too busy destroying himself.

The echoes roll the sky like thunder. The ground shakes and all the birds take flight. And I lie there, sinking into the earth as he pounds the stone with the hammer until there's nothing left.

Better

by Fredrick Obermeyer

Michael Kalderson screamed as he struggled to pass a kidney stone. Excruciating pain burned through his back, kidneys, and down the length of his urethra.

Sweat stood out on his forehead and his stomach twisted with nausea. He groaned and sagged against the bathroom wall, wishing that he could just die right then and there.

Why does all this have to happen to me? Michael thought.

He had never had much good luck in his life; it seemed like he was a walking shit magnet, attracting all the world's troubles into his orbit. The kidney stones were just the latest incident in a seemingly endless string of bad luck.

Without warning, saliva filled Michael's mouth and nausea overwhelmed him. He doubled over and vomited, the acid burning his mucus membranes. Coughing, he sat on the toilet for a few minutes, his throat and mouth aching. Feverish pain stabbed his back every few seconds.

"Come on, you miserable fuck!" Michael said, staggering back to his feet. "Get out of my—"

His words broke off into another frenzied scream as volcanic agony burst through his penis. The pain was so sharp and sudden that he lost his breath. He grunted and pissed out a small stream of blood and urine, followed by two tiny stones. They made a clinking noise as they landed on the toilet's edge and fell into the water.

Still aching, Michael dropped to the floor and lay there in a heap, shaking and sobbing. The nearby grandfather clock chimed once.

One o'clock. He had to be at work in eight hours. More than anything, he wanted to take a sick day, but he had used them all up. He had to go to work or he would lose his job.

He flushed the toilet and went back to bed. The pain in his back and kidneys continued to torment him, making sleep nearly impossible.

♦

Half-asleep from his rough night, Michael staggered into the Tucson real estate office where he worked. As he entered, he checked his watch. He was already running a half-hour late, thanks to his car breaking down on the highway.

He trudged over to his cubicle to begin work, but when he arrived, he found that all his paperwork had been put into cardboard boxes.

Joe Garland, his manager, emerged from the back office and walked over. He was a short, plump man with rimless eyeglasses and a face like a sad bulldog.

Michael's lips quivered. "I'm fired, aren't I?"

Joe nodded and shrugged. "I'm sorry, Mike. I really don't want to do this to you, but the call came down from the main office this morning. We had to make some cuts and, uh …" His voice trailed off.

The awfulness of the day suddenly slammed into him like a freight train. Michael dropped his briefcase on the desk, covered his face with both hands and started crying.

"Come on, Mike. Let's go into my office and talk. It'll be alright."

Joe put his hand gently on Michael's shoulder and led him towards the office. The other realtors stared at him along the way. Michael's face reddened; it felt like the time he shit his pants on the jungle gym when he was five.

He bowed his head and let Joe lead him into the office.

Better

♦

All things considered, Joe was pretty nice. He gave Michael his last paycheck and promised to give him a good reference and severance pay. He even offered him a couple of job leads. Grateful for the man's kindness, Michael took the check and leads, then gathered up the boxes from his desk, left the office, and trudged down the street to the nearest bus stop.

As he walked, rain began pouring down from the sky. It almost never rained in the desert, so it was the perfect end to an awful day.

Michael laughed bitterly, tears stinging his already puffy eyes. The boxes he was carrying quickly got soaked. A small bus stop with a covered booth stood nearby.

If I can just make it there, I'll be fine, he thought.

He sprinted towards the booth, but halfway there, he slipped on the wet concrete. The boxes flew out of his hand and crashed to the ground, sending his stuff everywhere. As he fell, he struck the curb with his right knee. A loud, sickening crack filled the air, and Michael shrieked and tumbled off the sidewalk.

He landed face first in the gutter, with filthy, garbage-strewn water splashing over his face. He tried to pull himself back onto the sidewalk, but the pain forced him back down and he lay moaning in the runoff until an ambulance arrived.

♦

Two months later, Michael sat alone in his living room with a bottle of scotch. The car had been repossessed and he had sold all his furniture just to keep his place. It wasn't enough. The bank was going to foreclose soon, and he'd be out on the street. He had tried multiple times to find another job, but everybody kept saying "No."

Finally, it had reached the point where Michael didn't give a shit anymore. He just wanted to be left alone with his bad luck.

As he took a sip from the bottle, the doorbell rang. Michael ignored it and continued drinking, relishing the burn in his throat. The doorbell rang two more times.

"God damn it!" Michael bolted up from the chair. As he did, he lost his grip on the bottle and it shattered on the floor, spraying booze all over his feet. "Fucking son of a bitch!"

He staggered forward and stepped on one of the glass shards. Michael screamed and crashed into the opposite wall. The doorbell rang again.

"Oh for Christ's sake, open the fucking door yourself!" he yelled. Trailing blood, he limped over to the front door, unlocked it and threw it open. His friend Dwight Landillo was standing there, holding a brown paper bag that smelled like egg drop soup, fried rice, and General Tso's Chicken.

"Hey, buddy," Dwight said. He frowned and looked Michael over. "Are you alright?"

"Oh, I'm just fucking great, Dwight. I lost my job, I lost my car, I'm about to lose my house, and oh yeah, I've got a glass shard in my foot."

"Well, I came over because I wanted to talk to you about something."

"What?"

"If you let me in, I'll tell you."

♦

After Dwight tended to Michael's foot, they sat down in what remained of his dining room. Since Michael didn't have a table, chairs, or a carpet anymore, they had to dine on the floor.

Dwight laid out the Chinese food with some paper plates and wooden chopsticks, then reached into his coat pocket and took out a small silver tin.

"I was debating whether or not to tell you about this, but I figured you needed some help." Dwight opened the tin to reveal several small white pills within.

"What are those?" Michael said, gobbling down a chunk of chicken. "Cyanide?"

"Nope," Dwight said. "They're called Better."

"Better what?"

"Just Better."

Michael swallowed the chunk and nearly choked on it. He coughed a couple of times, then put his chopsticks on the plate.

"I don't understand," he said.

"You know how I've always seemed to have good luck recently?" Dwight said.

"Yeah."

In fact, it almost seemed as if his life were too good. A few months ago, Dwight had as much bad luck as Michael. He had ended up in the hospital with a gallbladder infection, his wife had cheated on him with the local elementary school principal, and the IRS was about to nail him for tax evasion. Then everything had turned around for the better, almost overnight.

"This is the reason." Dwight closed the tin. "A good friend gave it to me."

"What's his name?"

Dwight laughed nervously. "I'd rather not say. My supplier likes to remain anonymous."

"I'm sure he does." Michael gestured to the tin. "So what do these mystery pills do?"

"It might sound crazy, but Better is a good-luck drug."

"Get the fuck out of here!"

"I'm not bullshitting you, man." He held out the tin. "Take one and see for yourself."

"No."

"What've you got to lose? Your life's already in the shitter, anyway."

Michael stared at the tin. "What's in it?"

"I told you, good luck."

"Yeah, right. How's it made?"

"It's a trade secret. The FDA hasn't officially approved it."

"So it's illegal, then."

"What do you care if it's illegal? Did that ever stop you from smoking weed?"

Michael shook his head.

"So quit being a baby and take one." Dwight took out a pill, popped it his mouth, and swallowed. "See, it's safe." He took out another pill and held it out to Michael. "Here, just take one."

"Thanks, but no thanks."

"Suit yourself. I'm only trying to help." He slid the tin back into his pocket, then continued eating. "So when do you get evicted?"

"A week from today," Michael said.

"Do you want to stay with me?"

He considered it. Dwight lived in a large mansion on the outskirts of Tucson, but Michael had never been comfortable with charity.

"That's alright."

"Well the offer's still open if you want it."

"Thanks, but I'm looking at some more job ads. I'll find something."

It was bullshit, of course. The only thing Michael was really looking at was a fresh bottle of scotch.

♦

Later that night, Michael woke up to a sharp pain in his kidneys. He groaned and clutched his aching back.

Better

Not again, he thought.

He grabbed his crotch and limped to the bathroom. On the way there, he noticed Dwight's tin of Better lying on the dining room counter. The bastard had left it there behind an empty bottle.

Michael hobbled over to it and looked at it.

Don't do it, he thought.

Another bolt of pain struck him. He shouted and doubled over in agony, wondering if this kidney stone was going to kill him.

Could this really improve my luck? he thought. *No, he's bullshitting me.*

Burning pain burst through his kidneys like a rocket, making him yell. He limped to the bathroom and tried to pass the stone, but it wouldn't come.

Wracked with pain, he lurched back to the dining room counter.

Fuck it! Michael thought. *I'll just take one.*

He took out a pill and swallowed it. Nothing happened.

So much for good luck, Michael thought.

He hobbled back to the bathroom. For the next ten minutes, he tried in vain to pass the stone, but it wouldn't come.

Great, he thought. *Now I'll have to go to the ER and rack up another bill.*

He started to walk out of the bathroom when a comforting warmth rushed through his body. Slowly, the agony in his penis and kidneys began to subside.

After another ten minutes in front of the toilet, the pain almost disappeared completely. Michael passed several kidney stone shards through his urethra along with some blood, and sighed with relief as he flushed the toilet.

Once he finished, he climbed back into bed and immediately fell asleep.

♦

A ringing phone woke Michael the next morning. He snatched it up.

"Yeah?"

"Is this Mr. Michael Kalderson?" a male voice said.

"Who's this?"

"My name is Gerald Haskovitz; I'm an attorney with Martin, Haskovitz and Gorschet."

"What do you want?"

"I'm afraid I have some bad news for you."

Michael groaned. *So much for this Better drug working*, he thought.

"I'm afraid your Aunt Sarah died last Thursday," Haskovitz said. "I'm very sorry for your loss."

"Sarah who?" Michael said.

"Sarah Goldwin, your great-aunt. Don't you remember her?"

"Vaguely." He had only visited Aunt Sarah twice when he was a kid; she hadn't gotten along too well with his parents. "Why are you calling me?"

"Well, I'm the executor of her will, and as it turns out, she left you quite a lot. If you can come down to Dallas for the reading this Friday, we can handle all the details."

Michael's eyes bolted open. "Of course."

"Very good, Mr. Kalderson. I'll see you then." Haskovitz hung up.

Maybe this drug really does work, Michael thought.

♦

That week, Michael inherited over three million dollars from Aunt Sarah's bank account, along with stocks, bonds, T-bills, and 400 acres of prime real estate in Texas and Oklahoma. After taxes and legal fees, he stood to earn more than two hundred million dollars.

When Michael returned home, he splurged big time. He took

himself out to eat at Tucson's most expensive restaurant, bought himself a brand-new convertible and leather furniture, and paid off the mortgage on his house.

He supposed that he should feel guilty for benefiting from Aunt Sarah's death, but she had no other next-of-kin and he had hardly known her anyway.

Now that he had lots of money and free time, Michael decided to take a trip to the Bahamas to get some sun and surf.

♦

After taking his daily dose of Better, Michael reclined in a deck chair on the cruise ship *Tyche* and enjoyed the bright morning sunlight and the glorious sight of the endless ocean.

As he relaxed, a beautiful young woman in a pink bikini sat down in the deck chair next to him. She had long, black hair and large breasts. Michael sighed happily as he stared at her glorious cleavage.

The woman turned to him and said, "Could you do my legs for me?"

"Sure," Michael said.

He took her bottle of suntan lotion and began applying it to her legs. He slid his right hand slowly up her leg towards the edge of her bikini bottom, but he stopped a few inches below her firm butt.

The woman smiled. "Like what you see?" she said, wiggling her bottom.

"No. I love it."

She laughed. Michael handed her back the bottle.

"I'm Michael Kalderson."

"Tanya Palmer. Nice to meet you." They shook hands.

"First time in the Bahamas?"

"No, I've been here once before," Tanya said.

"Oh really. Did you like it?"

"No." She lay back. "I loved it."

Michael chuckled. "So are you by yourself?" he said, glancing around.

"For the moment."

"What are you going to do when you get to the island?"

"Whatever I want." She rubbed her breasts and smiled. "Do you have anyone with you?"

"Nope."

"Looking for some company?"

"Are you offering?"

She smiled mischievously. "Maybe." She held out the squirt bottle. "If you do my arms."

"With pleasure."

♦

Two weeks later, Tanya moved into Michael's house. He helped her bring in most of her stuff and set her up in his bedroom. At night, they would make love and stay up until the early morning hours, watching TV, playing chess, and cooking meals together.

Tanya was a trust-fund baby whose parents owned stock in several major construction firms. When he asked what she did, she said, "Whatever I want."

Michael bought a gym set and began working out. And as the weeks went on, he noticed that his slight pot belly quickly turned into a six-pack. He had a ton of money in the bank, and best of all, he had Tanya.

Life was perfect. Maybe a little too perfect. He grew nervous, wondering if he was becoming addicted to Better.

On a whim, he stopped taking it one day. For the first two days, nothing bad happened, but on the third, he slipped on the tub and banged his bad knee. He cried out and fell to the floor, nearly breaking his neck in the process. As he limped up, Tanya rushed in and accidentally banged his head against the door.

"Ow!"

"Are you alright?" Tanya said.

"No," Michael said. "I banged my knee. Shit, it fucking hurts!"

"Here, let me get you to the bed."

She helped him limp into the bedroom and laid him down on the bed. Moaning, he looked up at her. Part of him wanted to tell her about Better, but he didn't want to ruin their relationship or make her think worse of him.

"Just relax. I'll be back with some ice."

Michael sighed. While she was gone, he reached into his night table for his stash of Better. Dwight had been supplying him with the pills for weeks now. He hesitated for a moment, but then he took a tablet.

After he put the tin away, he wondered, *Where does this stuff come from, anyway?* Just as Tanya entered the room, he hid the pill container. *I'll have to ask Dwight about it.*

He doubted that his friend would tell him.

♦

Michael sat with Dwight on the patio of his friend's mansion, looking out at the cragged Tucson skyline.

"Sorry, buddy, like I said, it's a trade secret," Dwight said.

"Come on, man," Michael said. "You can tell me."

"I said 'No.' Now stop asking questions."

"What if I stop taking it?"

"That's your choice. But don't be surprised if your life turns to shit again."

Michael sighed.

♦

Curious about Better's composition, Michael sent a pill from Dwight's next batch to an independent laboratory. A week later, the results came back: it was a sugar pill.

It can't be a placebo, Michael thought. *My luck's been too good.*

Needing an answer, Michael decided to follow Dwight. He told Tanya that he was going out on a business trip for a week and left her in charge of the house, then he rented a car and began tailing Dwight.

The first three days brought no results, but on the fourth, Dwight left Tucson and drove out to the Arizona–Mexico border.

Michael followed his friend to a compound located deep in the desert. The property was surrounded with a chain-link fence with a sign that read, "PRIVATE PROPERTY. DO NOT ENTER." Several concrete buildings lay inside the compound.

Michael slowed his car a few hundred feet from the edge of the property, grabbed a pair of binoculars from the glove compartment, and looked out. Dwight stopped his car at the gate, flashed his ID at the guard stationed there, and got waved through.

What the hell are you doing, Dwight? Michael thought.

Michael parked his car a few hundred feet down the road, got out, and crept up to the southern side of the compound fence, which didn't appear to be monitored. Unsure if the fence was electrified, he tossed a stone at it. Nothing.

He drove away from the compound, went to a tool shop in a nearby town and bought wire cutters, then returned to the fence an hour later.

He cut his way through the links and crawled onto the property. Beyond the fence, he crept low and darted past two narrow concrete buildings. At the third building, he ducked behind a metal dumpster and looked around.

Dwight's car was parked outside the largest building on the compound along with several other vehicles, including two tractor-trailers. Sodium lamps were located in several spots around the property, illuminating the whole area.

Michael started to head out when a fat security guard with a gun and walkie-talkie waddled in his direction. Michael threw himself back behind the dumpster, waited for the guard to pass, and darted out across the open space to the largest building, staying out of the light.

When he arrived at the farthest corner of the building, he heard several voices coming from inside, but he couldn't understand them. Since there were no windows on the first floor, he climbed onto a dumpster and peeked inside the building through a second-floor window.

At least a hundred Hispanic and Asian people were strapped to cots that had been bolted to the floor. They were all unconscious with copper-colored, pyramid-shaped apparatuses attached to their heads. Each apparatus had tubes and needles implanted in various spots on each person. The devices were draining some kind of clear fluid that collected into large metal tanks nearby.

Occasionally, men entered the building, disconnected and unstrapped people, then carried them out to another building across the lot.

"If you wanted a tour, you could've asked," Dwight said.

Michael gasped and looked behind him. Dwight was standing with five security guards, all pointing pistols at him. Trembling, Michael frowned and looked over their shoulders at the gate.

"Please don't do anything heroic," Dwight said. "I'd hate to have the boys do something unpleasant."

Michael sighed. "Alright, I'll come quietly."

He hopped down from the dumpster. As soon as he hit the ground, the guards yanked his arms behind his back and handcuffed him.

They led Michael across the compound and into one of the trailers. Inside, there were several desks with laptop computers, chairs, charts, and other office equipment. The place smelled of old coffee and lemon varnish.

"Give me the keys and wait outside," Dwight said.

The security guards did as Dwight ordered and left the room. Dwight came over and unlocked Michael, then sat back behind the desk.

"I trust you won't be stupid enough to try anything," Dwight said.

"I guess you're making Better from those people in that building." Michael said.

"That's right. We bring immigrants in across the Mexican border—mostly Hispanics but some Asians, too—and into Baja California. Once we get them in the trucks, we put them to sleep, drain their good luck with the machines, convert it to pill form, and send it out to our clients."

Michael rubbed his sore wrists. "And then what?"

"Then we take care of them."

Michael frowned. "By take care of, do you mean …"

"No, we don't kill them. We put them back in the trucks, leave them in shacks a few miles from here, and let them go on their merry way. They get a shot at the American Dream and we get their luck. Everybody's happy."

"But their good luck is gone."

Dwight shrugged. "It comes back eventually."

"Do they even know what they're getting into?"

"We don't tell them about the process, but like I said, we don't kill them."

Shaken, Michael looked at Dwight. His friend's gaze was so steely that he couldn't tell if he was telling the truth or not.

"What about the police and the border patrol?" Michael said.

"Some of them are our best clients," Dwight said, "and we pay off the rest. If anybody gets suspicious …" Dwight chuckled and took out a Better pill. "We've got good luck on our side."

"Who set up this whole scheme?"

Better

"I can't tell you."

"Why not? Is it you?"

Dwight chuckled. "No way, man. I'm just one small fish in a very big pond."

"Then who's in charge?"

"You don't understand, do you? There's not just one person running the show. It's actually a huge, anonymous, multi-national conglomerate. They've got places like this set up all over the world."

"Well, it doesn't matter who runs this operation. We have to go to the authorities."

"Are you fucking crazy? If we give up Better, our lives will turn to shit again."

"But this isn't right!"

"Right?" Dwight laughed. "What's right? Who cares about siphoning good luck off a bunch of stinky foreigners? You think we're going to jeopardize this whole operation over your moral objections?"

"They're people, Dwight."

Dwight waved his hand. "Stop acting like such a fucking Boy Scout. We've been using them for decades as maids and laundry workers. Now we're just using them in a different way."

"I can't do this, Dwight." Michael shook his head. "It's not right."

"Before you do something stupid, let me give you a little heads-up." Dwight reached into his pocket and took out another tin. "We've been working on another pill for any problems that might crop up." He dumped out a yellow pill. "It's called Worse. We culled it from people who have rotten luck like we did."

Fear crept into Michael's chest, tightening the muscles there. Dwight reached under the table. Seconds later, the guards came in and held him down.

"What—"

"Be quiet and listen."

Michael froze in their arms.

"I noticed you following me that first day, and I knew you wouldn't give up till you had your answers. So I took the liberty of swapping out your Better with a much weaker dose so you couldn't get the drop on us," Dwight said. "Then I slipped Tanya some Worse right before I let you follow me out here."

Michael's heart stopped. "No."

Dwight took a smartphone out from his jacket and tapped the screen. A video appeared, showing Tanya in a hospital bed somewhere, intubated and hooked up to a ventilator.

"Three hours ago, a drunk driver hopped the sidewalk and hit her," Dwight said. "Now she's in a coma. Her chances of recovery are slim."

"God damn you!" Michael said. He tried to lunge for Dwight, but the men held him down.

"You have two options." Dwight reached into his pocket and laid a white pill next to the yellow one. "She could have a miraculous recovery or she could suddenly die." He gestured to the pills. "So what's it going to be, old buddy?"

"You fucking piece of shit!" Michael burst into tears and relaxed in their arms.

A facial tic made Dwight's cheek twitch. "If you choose the second option, I'm afraid you'll have to take Worse as well, and I wouldn't want that."

Frustrated, Michael nearly gave up, but he'd rather die than let Dwight win. He couldn't let Tanya go down with him, though.

"Give her the Better."

Dwight slapped the table. "I knew you'd see it my way." He dialed a number on the smartphone and said, "He chose Better," then hung up.

"So you'll kill me now," Michael said.

"No," Dwight said. "I want you to get Better." He nodded to one of the guards.

Better

Michael felt a prick on his shoulder. Moments later, he passed out.

♦

When he awoke in the desert three days later, the compound and its buildings had been totally stripped.

Michael returned home and listened to a voicemail message from the hospital saying that Tanya had experienced a miraculous recovery. The nurse claimed that Tanya was now completely stable, but Michael knew better. One mistake and she could die instantly.

He considered exposing the group, but what could he say? He was taking a good-luck drug? At best, they'd lock him up in a nuthouse. At worst, an undercover operative could give him and Tanya a lethal dose of Worse.

Frustrated, he went to the hospital to make sure Tanya was alright.

♦

One week later, Michael picked Tanya up from the hospital and drove her back home. As he helped push her wheelchair inside the house, he saw a sports car parked on the street in front of his house.

It was Dwight. He had a big, shit-eating grin on his face.

Michael sneered as he looked out the front door.

Dwight got out of his car and walked across the driveway towards them.

"Stay here," Michael said to Tanya.

He strode out of the house towards Dwight, balling up his fists. But before he could nail his former friend, Dwight swept Michael up in his arms, hugged him and said, "Easy there, good buddy. Share the love."

Michael tried to pull free and throw a punch, but his luck wasn't as good as it should have been. Dwight tripped him up and laid him out on the pavement.

"Relax. I come bearing gifts." Dwight let him go and took out a tin. "It's not nearly as strong as your former dose, and the luck is designed to wear out in less than a week, but it's enough to help you get by." He tossed it onto Michael's chest.

Michael licked his lips, wanting the Better. His kidney stones had been acting up again. However, he still remembered the compound and those people. Dwight and his conspirators were getting away with it, and there wasn't a thing Michael could do to stop them. At least, not yet.

He snatched the tin off his chest, stood and threw it right at Dwight's face. Dwight deflected the tin at the last moment with his hand, but it popped open and the pills went flying everywhere.

"Are you sure you want to do that?" Dwight said. "I'm only trying to help."

"Fuck off!"

"So be it." He waved to Tanya, then trotted back to his sports car and got in.

As Dwight started his car up, Michael rushed over to the passenger side and said, "Someday, Dwight."

Dwight smiled and sped down the street.

Michael shook his head and walked back up the driveway. Near the door, he saw a single tablet of Better lying on the concrete. A slight pain stabbed his kidneys and he groaned.

Michael reached down, picked up the tablet, and looked at it for a moment. Hating himself, he tossed it in his mouth and swallowed.

Divine Organ
by Madeline Popelka

1. Haruspex: The Body is a Forecast

First, there was darkness. Then came a light, followed by the sputtering of a blue screen above Jake's eyes. There were two words on the screen: "Stay awake." Then came an angry shriek of pulsing metal. A short silence followed, then a tinny voice vibrated through the headphones.

"You doing okay, Jake?"

He almost nodded before he remembered they had told him to stay still. Even if he had wanted to move, a plastic harness kept his head tightly clamped to the narrow bed. He pressed the little green button they had given him to hold in his right hand.

"Great. Hang in there for ten more minutes and we'll be done with the scan."

Jake tried to let his mind drift. He didn't like enclosed spaces, and this narrow cylinder was feeling increasingly like a coffin. There was smooth plastic on all sides, and he could hear giant magnets gyrating noisily overhead, bombarding his brain with electromagnetic pulses. The noises were rhythmic, harsh, and alien.

To Jake, it sounded like the clicking and screeching of a large, ancient insect cornering a victim. For a moment, he imagined the vise holding his head was the pincer of a gigantic praying mantis with glassy, emotionless eyes considering his pulverization.

After a while, the scan ended.

♦

"Would you look at this resolution?" The doctor leaned over to show Jake the blue transparent sheet in his folder. He squinted at the image of his brain. The doctor was right; it was very clear, better than any image he'd seen on TV or the Internet.

"It's all that loud clicking near the end," the doctor said. "They figured out how to clean up the frequency and it really improved the images." He poked the image for emphasis. "We got the upgrade last month. The new tech was tricky to get the hang of, but it looks like the technicians got it worked out."

Jake could make out each inlet and valley in his brain, but it was the small white spot near the left side of his skull that drew his attention. The doctor noticed Jake's gaze and quickly rearranged his face into what he believed to be a sympathetic expression.

"Er, yes. I suppose you'd like to hear more about the tumor. As you can tell from the clean edges, it's benign. We don't see any of the malignant branching into the rest of the brain that would seriously concern us. It's also pushed up against the border of your skull, so the surgery will be relatively noninvasive. It's been pressing into your temporal lobe, which caused the headaches and memory issues. You're very lucky; these types of tumors have a high survival rate."

"That's good to hear," Jake said.

"We'll schedule the surgery for about a month from now. We'd have you in earlier, but the schedule is pretty tight and we need to prioritize the life-threatening cases. In the meantime, I recommend that you avoid driving, just in case you get another migraine on the road."

"I guess I'll take the bus back, then."

"Do you have anyone to pick you up?" The doctor narrowed his eyes. "I always forget, are you guys allowed to get married?"

Jake forced himself to smile. "Of course. That's mostly just Catholics."

"Right. And your church is … ?"

"Unity Church of Christ, down on Third Avenue. I guess you would call us Protestants, but we're more about community than labels. Everyone's welcome. If you'd like to come to our service Sunday, it's—"

"Oh, no," the doctor interjected. "Thanks for the offer, but Marie's family is Jewish and we generally like to avoid that whole scene." He glanced at his watch. "You know what, Jake? I've got another appointment I have to get to, but I'll call you for the surgery consultation. Have a safe ride home."

With a firm hand on Jake's back, the doctor propelled him back out into the waiting room.

♦

Jake checked his phone as he was leaving the hospital. He had missed a call from Ms. Veras, the woman who volunteered at the church doing secretarial work. She probably wanted to type up his notes for the sermon on Sunday. On the bus, he texted her to let her know he'd be late.

Ms. Veras could be helpful to a fault, lingering over his shoulder while he worked in his office, her face as hopeful as a lost puppy's. Her willingness could be overwhelming at times, but the church was not in a position to refuse volunteer help.

Back at home, Jake tried to get the sermon down on paper, but his fingers were shaking. His ears were still buzzing from his time in the scanner, and he couldn't stop envisioning the image of his own mind, two-dimensional and smudged with disease. He thought it was strange to live in a body for a lifetime and have so little control over its depths.

When he was a child, there had been a forest behind his home that sprawled beyond his family's property. He often played along the edges, but once, he ventured too far into the woods. With his house out of sight, he became disoriented and lost track of the way home.

The trees, once so familiar to him, became cold and unyielding.

Jake had only been eight at the time, and his fright quickly reduced him to tears. He had collapsed, exhausted, onto a bed of pine needles. He awoke some time later in the strong arms of his father, who carried him to safety.

Feeling similarly lost, Jake sat down to write his sermon. During the MRI, he'd resorted to prayer to quell his fears. It had given him the seeds of a new sermon, but he needed to check the scripture first. He flipped open the Bible he used most frequently. The second half was heavy with bookmarks, but he flipped to the earlier chapters, trying to find the parable that had been tugging at his mind.

As a child, he had held a fondness for the story of Jacob, his namesake. Now he turned the pages to the story. A verse caught his eye: "Balaam blessed Jacob, and he did not resort to divination, but turned his face toward the wilderness … the Spirit of God came and spoke his message …"

Jake copied this line down on a fresh page of his notes. At the top he titled it:

"Trust the messengers that God sends you."

He copied down a few more lines until he was satisfied, the he transcribed them onto his computer and emailed them to Ms. Veras. She'd have it ready for Sunday's church bulletin.

Soon after, Jake retired to bed. Although he was exhausted, it was hours before his mind was calm enough fall unconscious.

♦

2. Exegesis

Jesus's robes were purple. So was his face. In fact, it was beginning to look like his arms, legs, and sandals would also be purple. Rachel Veras watched, her lips pursed, as Joey Volkmann drowned the Lord Jesus in a sea of purple, refusing to share the Unity

Divine Organ

Church's copy of the New Testament Coloring Book with the other children at the table. Rachel found most of the children to be delightful, but there was something about Joey that made her itch with rage. Perhaps it was the moronic way he held his mouth open as he drew.

She was just about to tell Joey to give it a rest and play with some blocks for Christ's sake, when she noticed Pastor Jake heading over to check on her. It would not do to have the Pastor see her being impatient with children. Rachel's sister had told her that men were always subconsciously judging women on their caretaking abilities, so she tousled Joey's hair and turned toward the Pastor, smiling.

"Hello, Pastor. How are you?"

"I'm fine, Ms. Veras, thanks for asking. I can't tell you how much the parents appreciate you watching over the kids during the coffee hour."

"Well, they don't cause any trouble."

Joey had taken to smearing a single zigzag line of purple on each page of the book, rendering several illustrations of the crucifixion useless. Rachel dug her nails into her palms but kept her attention on the Pastor.

"That was an interesting sermon you gave today," she continued. "I had no idea about all that King of Babylon business."

"Yes, I think many of us struggle with interpreting God's message. In many places, the Bible forbids divination and interpreting omens, but some of his favorite prophets relied on pagan practices to speak with him."

"I try to stay away from all that. It's so confusing!"

"Well, as I said, it can be confusing to try and understand the messages God sends us in times of trouble. But sometimes, the most unlikely events are how he speaks to us. We just have to be willing to listen."

Joey had begun to tear out several unused sheets depicting the Last

Supper. He worked with emotionless conviction, a single string of snot hanging precariously from his chin.

"You mentioned you had a doctor's appointment Friday?"

The Pastor's mouth tightened. "Yes, well, they found a tumor in my head. It's very small and not life-threatening. I have an operation scheduled for sometime next month."

"Oh, no! I'm sorry you have to go through that."

"I'll be absolutely fine, don't worry."

Rachel was uncomfortable. She had been working up the courage to ask the Pastor to dinner for months. This was not an ideal moment, but her sister had made her swear she'd ask today.

"Well, since you're going through so much, I was thinking that—"

Joey began scrawling directly on the table, an insult Rachel could not bear, even for the Pastor. She reached down, yanking his arm away.

"Joey, you can't do that! Coloring time is over."

The Pastor checked his watch. "Coffee hour is just about over, too. I should get going."

"Wait!" She grabbed at his hand as he turned away. It was colder than she had expected. "Would you like to come over for dinner tonight?"

He smiled at her, but his eyes were vacant.

"Thank you, Ms. Veras, but I think it'd be best if we both kept our focus on the community, where we can do the most good."

Rachel's heart plunged.

"But don't fret, dear. Someone will come along soon enough, and you'll forget all about me." He took his hand out from under hers and patted her head. Then he did the same to Joey. "See you next week!"

Rachel's face was burning as she watched the Pastor leave. Beside her, Joey stuffed the remainder of the purple crayon into his mouth. She was too disheartened to stop him.

Divine Organ

◆

3. Mantis, the Prophet

There are many women named Rachel, but she was the first. She was remembered as a wife, yet she lived as a hunter. In another world, they called her Artemis. In this little village with a desert to the south and pinewoods to the north, she was tracking her prey. It was early in the morning; the sun had only just begun to stain the sky a predawn teal.

That night, a seraph had appeared in her bedroom, awaking only her. The six-winged angel hovered in the air, its face and body hidden behind a flurry of ever-shifting silver feathers. The seraph told her to track and kill a deer for the Lord. It spoke to her without sound, its message transmitting directly into her mind.

Nodding her assent, she disentwined from the sleeping form of her husband. He had dealt with his fair share of angels in his own time, but this was her trial. Silently, she slipped out of the house and took to the woods with her bow. Keeping her eyes to the ground, Rachel quickly uncovered a fresh set of deer prints, less than a day old. She followed the trail for several hours until the sun rose.

Finally, she arrived in a clearing. A small halo of wild grass had been pushed down where the deer had rested for the evening. Rachel traced the perimeter, but she could not find a set of prints leading away. The trail of the deer had vanished. Perplexed, she lay down in the nest, trying to sense with her fingers a slight indent in the grass, anything that would indicate the departure of the creature.

Suddenly, she heard the fluttering of wings above her. She looked up to see the seraph land. It unwound the wings that covered its face and body. With a growing sense of unease, Rachel reached for her bow, only to realize she couldn't move her limbs. The seraph's wings glinted in the morning light. They shone metallically, in a way Rachel hadn't noticed before. A moment too late, she realized that the wings were sharp as knives. The seraph serenely slid a wing down and along her body. She was powerless to resist as it lacerated her abdomen.

The green, compound eyes of the seraph stared dispassionately down at her. Rachel knew that the seraph covered itself to shield against the divinity of the Lord, and seeing its face for the first time, she realized it was because their many-faceted eyes could not blink. It opened its pincered mouth and unleashed a cacophony of electronic, rhythmic clacking that shocked Rachel into a seizure. Eventually, her heart stopped and her vision cleared.

In death, Rachel's eyes were open, and she watched as a second profile appeared above her. It was the angel Azazel, unadorned and frail, with weathered, tan skin. He bent down to her, his joints cracking. He reached into her and gently removed her liver. He felt along the organ, examining the spots and scars as a crone would read the palm of a hand. Then he spoke:

"The surgery must happen now. Their machine has misread the omens. Without haste, the priest will die within the year."

The seraph nodded its triangular head and departed. Azazel held the dripping liver and gazed into Rachel's eyes for the first time. Then he reached down to gently close her eyelids.

♦

Rachel Veras lurched awake in her bed. She felt her dream tugging at her, dark and full of portent. The beating of wings echoed in her ears. There had been a sign, something that Rachel needed to remember, something about the Pastor. She was gripped with a terrible urgency to write down a phrase she could barely remember. Already the edges of her dream were fading.

As she reached for a notebook on her bedside table to write down her dream, the memory of her shame with the Pastor from the previous day flooded her head. How childish she would look, coming to him with a dream after he had rejected her. She'd seem like a lovesick teenager that couldn't take a hint. Surely she was being irrational. She left the notebook blank and returned to an uneasy sleep.

Rachel told no one of her dream. In the following weeks, she spent less time at the church and shushed her sister whenever she mentioned the Pastor. Rachel told herself that this was a better life. Two months later, when the Pastor stood at the podium with shadows under his eyes and stitches in his shorn head, she was consumed with a dreadful sense of vindication.

At the funeral, she found she could not cry. That night she dreamed again, this time of a smooth, curved coffin that was buried deep beneath the earth's tectonic plates. In it she was trapped, paralyzed, as the screech of electronic clicking crept ever closer.

◆◆◆

Settled

by Julio Toro San Martin

What was the name? For the life of her, she couldn't remember. She'd thought highly of the exhibit and the work of art, but now, funnily, couldn't remember its name.

She knew it had been somewhere on exhibit in London before the war. Then, when the Nazi bombs started falling, it had been moved to a private collection outside the city.

At the end of the war, her husband had found it amid the ruins. Apparently, relocation hadn't saved it from the bombs. After numerous thorough inquiries, no owner was found, so he had it shipped to the States.

Well, she wasn't about to drop the conversation just because she couldn't remember the name. Already, Alice had moved on to another topic, yet Mona wanted so much to show her the thing.

Looking outside, Mona listened to the wind blowing the unsettled yellow and orange leaves that had fallen from the trees, and in dim autumn's wake, felt the slowly encroaching cold and greater oncoming darkness, far removed from summer's sultriness.

If she wanted to show Alice, she would have to do it quickly, in case Alice decided to leave earlier than usual because of the weather.

"The pumpkins this year," Alice said, "are smaller than last year's crop. I've searched all around, but one really must go to the countryside to shop for the best ones, don't you think?"

"I really don't know about that sort of thing," Mona answered. "When I was younger, my father and older brothers and sisters took care of the shopping, and now that I'm married, Mr. Macready does the buying for pumpkins." She paused for a second, then continued in a lighter tone, "My, but you did say we get a lot of traffic here during Halloween, didn't you?"

"Oh, yes!" Alice said, barely containing her enthusiasm. "It's a regular fair around here. The children come from all parts looking for candy. You do give out candy and enjoy it—Halloween, I mean?"

"I suppose," Mona said. "Now that the boarder's gone and Mr. Macready won't be getting back from Europe for some time, I'll have to do something to keep away the boredom. Yes, I think I will give out candy."

Mentioning how alone she was brought back a slight twinge of the depression she had been feeling. With Mr. Macready working in London as a building contractor and the boarder, his business at the university now finished, back home in the Southwest, it was only Alice, dear Alice, and her frequent visits—except recently, when she'd gone on vacation—which provided Mona with at least some company.

When she'd moved here with her newlywed husband from Alabama, she hadn't expected this to come about: no husband, no children, no job and no expectation of finding one, and no friends, except for Alice and a handful of acquaintances who rarely visited, if ever. It was enough to drive any sane person to depression and to cling onto any scrap of companionship that could be found.

So when Alice said she was leaving, Mona wouldn't have it. Besides, she hadn't yet shown Alice the exhibit piece her husband had sent her.

"Oh, Alice, must you go?" Mona asked. "Can't you stay for supper?"

"If it will make you feel better, I can stay a while longer."

"Oh, it most definitely will! You can help me cook!" Mona said, her face brightening. "But first, do let me show you the exhibit piece. It's a simply marvelous thing. They say it was made by an artist in the

'30s. He was said at the time to be absolutely, deliciously deranged. But isn't that what they say of all true geniuses, dear Alice?"

She led Alice to the basement door.

"We keep it down here. It's much larger than you would imagine. I feel rather ashamed, but I can't remember the piece's name for the life of me. As I've said, it was rather popular during the '30s. I really can't go on showing you without sharing any real information with you. Do wait for me while I go search for one of the newspapers that Mr. Macready sent me along with the piece. Its name and more of its history is in them."

Alice opened the door and turned on the stairway lights.

"My, but you're in a hurry!" Mona said. "Though you have been a dear, offering to stay until after supper. Do you want to go on ahead and wait for me downstairs? Very well, do mind your step on the way down while I go search for that paper. I shouldn't be more than a few seconds."

Alice walked briskly down the steps and stopped at the bottom, since the rest of the basement was still in darkness. Not wanting to waste too much time, she decided to go on ahead, feeling in the darkness for the overhead pull-chain light switch.

From upstairs, she heard Mona yelling clearly.

"I do appreciate you staying, Alice. You can't imagine how depressing this time of year can be for someone without company. I suppose it can be a time of quiet contemplation for others, but not for me. I think it's simply beastly. The days getting shorter, the outside world emptying of people, the colors growing dullish and gray, everything dying and slowly turning cold like the inside of a bland, frozen refrigerator. It's beastly!"

After groping and almost giving up, Alice found the chain and pulled it. The overhead light bulb lit up spectacularly, forcing the blackness to retreat a short distance away.

She was surprised at how large the basement was! There were still vast sections in darkness. In a corner, she saw two pairs of ripped up men's shoes, neatly placed side-by-side. For some reason she couldn't quite grasp, she found the display deeply strange and unsettling.

Mona's voice was coming closer.

"The newspaper says the piece was originally on display in Southwark Street, London. It's a representation of an obscure totem creature from Nome, Alaska, based on some barely-known legend from the place. You can read about it all in more detail soon."

Alice noticed some kind of symbol in blood-red paint on a crossbeam above. This was all deathly strange. As she moved closer to the outer darkness, she thought she might be able to make out the outline of something hiding in the shadows.

Was it an elephant's trunk she had glimpsed? And three shiny glazed things, perhaps eyes or massive marbles, coming closer? There was definitely something in the darkness … moving.

She was turning to leave when something hit her hard across the head. Dizzying pain sent her sprawling to the ground. Looking up, she had just enough time to see Mona rushing across the basement and up the stairs, carrying a hammer in her hand, stopping only to turn off the lights.

In seconds, Alice was in total darkness, tasting blood on her lips. Something was slowly crawling or slouching toward her. Not sure what else to do, Alice started yelling for help.

"Help me! Someone, please! Mona! Help me! Anyone!"

She heard Mona upstairs, moving around in the kitchen and running water. Was she getting supper ready? Even after what had just happened? The kitchen radio blared on.

Suddenly, a terrible, fishy stench reached her nose, and horrible slopping sounds started to inch toward her. Whatever it was, she could tell that it was big.

All her bodily defenses told her to flee, so she got up and flung herself in the direction of the stairs with all her might. She crashed straight into them, banging herself up. Pain flashed across her shins and nose, yet she immediately got up and ran blindly up the stairs. Hammering into the door, she reached for the handle and tried desperately to twist it, but it wouldn't budge. The door was locked.

The sound of the Andrews Sisters singing on the other side blended with her own words as she screamed, "For God's sake, Mona, let me out! You can't do this! Frederick knows that I came to see you today! People will come here, you can count on that! What about my daughter? Think of her! I was supposed to go to Washington tomorrow to visit my brother, who's a Senator! Do you understand, Mona? He won't let this go! Oh please, Mona! Please!"

Mona calmly put down the knife she was using to chop vegetables for the chicken stew and made her way to the basement door, rather bored. She quickly began to chastise Alice.

"Do be a dear and hush now, Alice. All this fuss is just serving to make you all flustered. The thing in the basement, it … I know that I'm not myself lately, but … it gets inside your head, strange-like. You think they're your ideas. I can't explain it right; it's strange. Now do be a good dear and hush. I promise it won't hurt for long."

Alice heard as Mona went back to the kitchen and resumed cooking. She slowly slunk down by the door and began to weep uncontrollably.

From the bottom steps, something began to make its way up to her.

♦

Mona sat alone eating supper and lamented the fact she always ate alone. First the boarder hadn't come for supper anymore, then Mr. Macready, and now Alice. Outside, she saw the new-fallen night, heard the howling wind crashing against the window glass, and grew despondent about her lonesome predicament.

She hated this time of year, hated what it represented to the soul. She felt as fragile as a weathered leaf, like she would crumble if pressed too hard. She couldn't—wouldn't—forgive Alice for leaving her alone like this, just her and her supper.

At least the children and their laughter during Halloween would bring some jubilation to her world. Their ringing, merry voices carrying within them the promise of spring and regeneration, when all things are made new again after the death of autumn and winter, would bring her some joy. This was some happiness to look forward to, some companionship.

She'd most definitely have to invite some children into the house—perhaps for supper! It was definitely what it would want. She'd do this before hibernating for the winter, before turning herself off, before awaiting nothing but the spring, before dying temporarily, drowning herself in sorrow and drink.

The thing in the basement was quiet now. It usually did this after a feast. Mona sensed it in her head and was strangely calmed.

She got up and went to look for Alice.

"Are you done being dead yet?" she asked.

When she found Alice, she would pick her up and hang her on a coat rack and talk to her. It was simple to do, since the creature usually broke all its food's bones as it sucked sustenance from the inside. Then she'd have Alice all to herself.

She carefully unlocked the basement door and peered into the darkness. Alice lay in a heap in a corner. As she inched nearer, a hand reached out to grasp her ankle, and grabbing onto it, yanked hard. This couldn't be! Alice should have been dead!

Mona lost her balance and tumbled down, falling and hitting herself horribly against the steps. Her neck was twisted in a very awkward way.

Now, at the bottom of the steps, she waited calmly for her end. There was no fear, only expectation. The thing, subtly controlling her mind, didn't want her to struggle.

Mona gasped as hundreds of sucking filaments appeared from the dark and embraced and attached themselves to her. Then the gentle feeding began.

In flashes, Mona saw what the creature had seen in its long life. Dizzying planets swam before her. Uncountable acolytes praised and worshipped it on worlds now dead. She saw this and much more, and was astounded. But it wasn't to last.

Soon the squeezing and breaking began, and the mashing of her insides commenced. As she slowly felt her life leaving her, she finally remembered the thing's name. She thought this quite comical, quite deranged even. But of course, how could she have forgotten?

Its name was Ran-Tegoth.

♦

The well-dressed woman who boarded the airplane a week later was rather strange and yet distinguished, with an air of steely purpose about her. She sat in first class and wore dark glasses and extraneous makeup, as if to cover some unsightly blemishes. Most took her for a socialite.

She spoke of traveling to many places and of a brother she had, a Senator. No one guessed she was leaving her daughter and husband behind—her whole life, in fact—to start a new life. The only items she carried with her from her old life were a carry-on bag and a huge container in the plane's cargo hold.

The metal container was roughly the size of a small car. It was marked hazardous and dangerous and was not to be opened. The creature rested inside.

Alice was much more suited for its purposes. Mona could never have offered it much. She was already dead, even while alive. It needed something more vivacious, more adventurous, something with more opportunities to offer.

By 9:45 p.m., the plane was airborne, bound for Washington, D.C.

No one ever found the grotesquely punctured loose skin-bag thing that had been dumped inside the garbage can in front of the Macready residence—the thing which once had been Mona Macready.

♦♦♦

White-Out

by Sean Moreland

The night was star-punctured; the snow, luminous. Despite this, the dark beyond the arc of the pickup's headlights seemed as thick as tar to Adler. Armies of pine stood at shivering attention on both sides of the highway, their snow-laden shapes phosphoric in the glare of high beams.

His father had once told him that at the age of three, Adler had become upset that the snow at night was not black like the sky it fell from. The old man, now five years dead, had reassured him that the snow was the same white as the stars, because that's where it actually came from.

Intergalactic snow. His father always was full of shit. He might even have made up the whole story, just to convince Adler what a chickenshit he had been as a rugrat. That definitely sounded like the old man.

Adler remembered being enraptured by snowy nights as a boy. He'd loved the way snow looked powder-dry but turned wet as soon as you touched it. Night driving used to be like hyperspace, soaring through star-like streaks of onrushing snow. It was hard to believe he'd loved that, once.

Now, at 44, Adler was pretty fucking sick of snow. He'd seen too many snowfalls and hauled freight through too many blizzards. The magic was long gone.

"A snowfall," he opined to the strip of his face silhouetted in the rearview, "is a lot like a stripper: nice to look at, but you don't want to get stuck in it for long."

Fortunately, the snowfall had slowed to a light downdrift since his pickup had peeled out of the Duke's lot two and a half hours back, or maybe his trajectory had just driven him out of the storm. He hoped Toronto was still getting buried alive, though. Sharyl hated driving in the snow.

"Enjoy digging out your own driveway, Shay." The words hung heavy in the artificially heated air. Adler's mind leapt over the faceless army of men his nearly-ex-wife might have handy to throw snow for her. Or ready to give her a throw.

Sharyl could shake the goods and amp up the charm like nobody's business. She was 38, looked 25, and could still hook a man and reel him in faster than you could say "Hey, baby." Adler ought to know.

"A blow job for a snow job," he grunted, grabbing the rye bottle and slinging fresh heat down his throat.

Just shy of Callander, a few flakes were lazily sinking down. It must have come down hard and heavy earlier in the evening, though. Everything but the highway, with its thin drifts, was humped high with driven powder. Tree limbs sagged wearily under the dead, white weight. At least Highway 11 was half-decently plowed, for once.

"Or maybe," he muttered, "a snowfall is more like a marriage. Nice to look at, but cold and nasty once you … ah, fuck." He dropped the abortive analogy and filled his mouth with another slug of whiskey instead.

He'd been working on bad women bons mots for the last half-hour. It hadn't been funny to start with, and sure as hell wasn't funny now. Besides, Sharyl was a stripper, so the jokes basically wrote themselves.

"Drunk, doin' 120, and still borin' the shit outta yourself, asshole."

The truck's rusted tailpipe gave an angry cough, accompanied by a gray-white cloud, visible in the rearview mirror. A taller tree on the left bent forward, dumping a white load on the roadside as he rumbled by. He imagined that cough, rocking through the night-hushed woods, scaring the shit out of squirrels, deer, coyotes, maybe even a bear.

He grinned lopsided satisfaction at the thought—a fine "fuck you" to this silent night that hung over his head like a lead shroud. Even the rye and the thrum of the unspooling highway weren't cutting through the smother of self-pity tonight, so he stamped the gas, smashing down his hurt with the truck's throttle.

The truck was as cough-wracked and creaking as its driver, but its engine still gave a good push. Its scratched and rust-speckled hood was aglow with speed, or so it seemed to Adler, his foot guiding the speedometer up to escape velocity. He'd know how fast that was when he and the truck got there.

Sharyl had thrown his ass out four months back. Since then, he'd been living out of a cheap motel close to the Pearson airport. He'd been doing next to no business, legal or otherwise, and his miniscule savings were dwindling with the requisite drinking, doping, and lap dances at dives like Foxy's, the Hutch, or earlier tonight, the Dirty Duke.

But tonight had been all about business. He'd set up the exchange three days ago, worked out the details with both North Bay Davie and Jay, his latest Hamilton-based dispenser.

"Hell," he'd told Jay, "if you don't mind a little drive, meet me at the Duke, it's as good a place as any for a hand-off."

It was, too, probably by design: dark, anonymous, full of obviously snow-blown dancers, bouncers, and a mangy pack of drunk and extremely distracted men who didn't give a shit what you were passing under the table, as long as you bought drinks and didn't whip your dick out too conspicuously.

Davie would be pissed that he was flying high, but he could handle Davie, and in the hundreds of times that Adler had made the hop up to the Bay and back, he'd never once been stopped by a cop.

A triangular yellow sign flashed by, a cartoonish deer silhouetted on it in black with a halo of five little holes blown around it. Last time he'd been up this way, he was pretty sure there'd only been two. God bless trigger-happy, deer-hating assholes who couldn't shoot for shit.

Well, fuck Sharyl and fuck the snow. It really wasn't such a bad night, was it? Sliding down the mouth of the highway, rough rye sliding down his. The drink was doing the job, too, giving him that lovely hell-burn in his belly, mellowing into a pleasant heat as it reached his road-stiff extremities.

Adler dropped the half-empty bottle back in his lap and returned to his own idiosyncratic version of "In the Pines." Sucking deep on dry air courtesy of the truck's humming heater, he throated out the chorus continuously, drawing out the vowels into a trembling howl of maudlin fury with every repetition of "my girl."

He could almost hear the effect he was going for, and was close to hitting just the right pitch of urgent misery. He had half an hour to go until he hit Davie's shack on the far side of North Bay, and he aimed to just keep crowing until he got there, his slurred heart gushing from his dilated mouth.

His left hand clamped the wheel and his right dipped down and snatched the bottle, lifting it from the warm cradle of his crotch, bringing it to his waiting whistle, getting it wet enough to birth the next ululating refrain.

After he socked the bottle back in his lap, he passed a glowing green road sign reading, "NORTH BAY 10" and began to re-gargle "Where'd you sleep last night?" Then, a pale shape shot out from the dark and onto the road.

The impact jarred him bad enough, but it was his reflexive stamp on the brakes and hard-right jerk on the wheel that crushed him against the seatbelt and battering his head on the wheel. The truck and whatever it had struck shuddered, spun, and shrieked together.

The truck's skid, a ribbon of agonized rubber bisecting the highway, left it idling lengthwise, front wheels buried in the roadside plow-packed bank, rear wheels straddling right about where the center line would've appeared if it wasn't veiled by shifts of snow.

Adler groaned. His face was numb. His nose and lip were dripping, and his mouth felt flush with blood. The taste made his guts heave.

He'd barely seen it, but it wasn't a deer, he knew that. It didn't run right and the color was too light. It was too big for a coyote. A husky, maybe? Christ, maybe a timber wolf?

Adler coughed, shook his head, and killed the engine. The truck's left high beam thrust out into the dark, onto a wall of densely packed, snow-capped pines. The right headlight was gone, smashed out by the dog or whatever the hell he'd hit.

Adler muttered a curse, incoherent even to his own ears, and drew a few rapid breaths. His left hand fumbled with the door handle, his right with his shirt pocket, hunting for his elusive smokes.

He forced open the door's rusted hinges and stumbled out of the cab to stand, swaying like an ice-laden tree on the cracked asphalt, black where his wheels had stripped it of drifting snow.

He hawked a spray of rye, blood, and mucus; wiped his mouth on the back of his right hand; and then went for, and finally found, the smokes. He used his left hand to pluck one and stuck it between his lips. His right dropped down to look for a light, and squished obscenely into sopping wet denim.

Adler gave a surprised grunt, thought for a moment he might've pissed himself during the smash and startle, and was relieved to realize it was just rye. The bottled had gone ass end up and spilled all over him.

Adler squinted down the dark highway, scanning for the body. Must be dead, anyway, he reasoned—he'd been doing 120 easy, and it looked and felt like he'd smacked the poor fucker dead on.

He stomped a few yards to where the truck's sidelong skid marks started and peered out into the opaque wall of trees and snow. He listened intently for a whimper or mewl, any telltale sound of pain. He had a shotgun tucked behind the seat, half-buried by coffee cups and empty smoke packs. If the dog wasn't dead, he resolved, he'd put it out of its misery. He owed the damned thing that, at least. Adler was no bleeding heart, but it was fair to say he didn't leave any living thing to suffer needlessly, not if he could help it. The world was full enough of pain as it was.

He paused, his eyes straining. There were no lights along this stretch of highway, no headlights visible in the distance. The moon was a half-hidden slit tonight. The stars looked clear but didn't shed enough light somehow.

His ears strained, hissing due to hearing loss from so many rock bars or the almost inaudible sound of slowly drifting snow.

He thought, not for the first time, that the hushed hiss of winter nights like this must've been where the phrase "white noise" came from, the snow greedily swallowing sound. No cries of pain and no broken groans rose up from the white not-quite-silence.

Nope. Nothing. Not a whimper. Not a peep. Either the dog had up and snuck away—not likely—or it was tossed back into a snow-sealed grave in the roadside brush, already as dead as his truck's right headlight. Either way, nothing could be done about it now, Adler decided, dragging his lighter up out of his pocket. Where the spilled rye caused his jeans and shirt to wetly cling to him, the winter cold crept in painfully, and he shivered, lifting the lighter to his face.

He sparked the smoke and took a deep, freezing drag.

"Hey, pooch," he breathed, unable to distinguish between the cloud of breath that bore the words and the smoke that flowed with it, "if you're out there and you ain't dead, lemme know. Miles to go before I sleep and all that."

Another raw lungful and he turned back toward the truck. It waited, halfway off the highway, ticking softly to itself. It was dangerous leaving it like that. It was time to hit the road. Davie was probably already batshit wondering where he was. Davie always got tight-assed before a buy, even a casual arrangement like tonight's.

He crunched back to the asphalt, puffing hungrily, rolling his neck and shoulders, producing the expected popcorn sounds. He didn't feel whiplashed, but it was hard to say. His neck could be an unbending knot of pain by tomorrow. Maybe Davie had some painkillers at the cabin.

Shit, it was Davie. Sure he did.

Adler had nearly reached the driver's door when the sound he'd given up listening for finally came. It began as a low moan. It wasn't at all what he'd expected, and Adler whipped around to face it. His eyes tracked the treeline as the sound rose into a plaintive whine. He felt a different kind of cold stab his spine. The cry rose higher, finally culminating in a tremulous keen that sounded like an alien wind instrument.

It was no dog sound, that, and no coyote. The pitch was all wrong and too … articulate. A too-human sound, agonized but almost musical.

That's what a damned banshee would sound like, Adler thought.

He shuffled toward the trees where he estimated the sound had originated. It faded out, leaving only a lonely echo in his head.

Why didn't he keep a flashlight in the truck?

He whistled, and called out, "Hey, I wanna help ya. Where are ya?"

The sound came again, lower this time, as though beginning in his bones, a drone, thrum, or something like that, but it climbed quickly, pitch creeping to a melodic keen, trembling in his ears, causing his heart to kick and his hands to tremble.

He moved toward the sound, reaching the edge of the asphalt, where the thin drifts ended in a jagged bank of plow-packed snow. His unlaced boots crunched as he mounted the bank, squinting into the dark treeline, trying to find the source of the wounded song even as it fell off again into silence.

There, before the massive trunk of a pine whose top pushed back the stars, between a skeletal scaffolding of sumac and the strangely leafy limbs of two large and unfamiliar bushes, the snow was marred with an ample scattering of dark flecks.

Blood?

His frozen fingers let the butt of his smoke slip. The echo of that scream-song fought with his own harsh breath as his boots dug footholds. He was edging into that pattern of dark flecks. He could see that each was roughly the size of his index fingernail and regularly rounded.

Not blood spots, he thought. No, not blood spots, but berries. A spray of berries, fallen from these bushes with their jagged, waxy-looking leaves.

Crunching closer, he finally saw the creature. Its broken white form was thrown into an elusive contour in the snow. It had been tossed at least 12 feet from the edge of the road, where it must have smashed against the trunk of the giant pine. Adler was amazed that he could see no blood spattering the snow, just the litter of those berries, their redness muted into undistinguished darkness by the stars and heavy-lidded moon.

He leaned down to get a good look at it. It was about four to four-and-a-half feet long, and covered with straight, silky fur. It was uniformly white except for blotches of red on its mouth and paws. Its lanky body was bent; its forelegs had been hammered down into the snow. The rear legs lay parallel with the ground. At first, Adler thought its rear paws were smeared with blood, but then he realized they were tipped with long claws, the same dark red as the berries.

It was no coyote. The snout was too short; the head was vaguely triangular, resembling, if anything, a cat's. Yet it had long ears, one folded, half-hidden beneath its skewed head, the other flopped limply in the snow.

It was still; its eyes were closed. It didn't seem to be breathing.

Could it have produced the awful cry as it died?

Its mouth was open slightly, its impossibly long tongue a limp squiggle in the snow. Tongue, mouth, and teeth were all blood-dark. Adler could see them steaming faintly in the frigid air.

Its sleek body was clearly built for speed, and judging by its claws and teeth, it had used that speed more often for hunting than for fleeing.

It was sure as shit no animal he'd ever seen before, and it looked both inexplicably beautiful and extremely dangerous. The sight of it lying broken, its slender body all but swallowed by the snow, filled Adler with an ache he couldn't explain.

It was an accident. It was an animal. Yet he felt like he'd struck and killed a child.

Without thinking, he knelt, barely aware of the pain in his bruised knees as they dented the dense snow. He stretched out his right hand to touch the creature's side, trying to feel breath, a heartbeat, something.

His fingers sank to the first knuckle into the creature's warm, white fur. It lay unresponsive under his touch, and he slid his hand along its still side. He felt the shift of shattered ribs, but no heartbeat, no breath. Nothing.

He leaned lower, looking closely at the blank shutters of its eyes. They were laced with white, delicate lashes. Sharyl would've killed for lashes like that, had spent untold time and money trying to fabricate them, not to mention the long red claws that, garish on her, only amplified the deadly beauty of the white beast.

The worst, though, was the parted mouth, its unfurled ribbon of tongue a red letter, illegible against a blank page.

The wet heat on his face, turning almost instantly to frost, told Adler he was crying. Without knowing why, without even knowing he was doing it, he laid his head down on the still creature's soft white side and began to convulsively weep. He lay there for an indeterminate stretch of time, wracked with a grief worse than any he'd felt before.

The intensity of the cold began to bring him back to some semblance of himself. The heat was already leaving the creature's body. Adler's face and hands felt frostbitten. He clambered to his feet, swaying on half-numb legs.

"What the fuck?" he sighed. He felt like shit that he'd killed this thing, sure. Hell, he felt more broken up about this than he did when his own mother died of cancer two years before. But life goes the fuck on, he swore at himself silently. He couldn't just lie down and die here with it, whatever it was.

"Miles to go before I sleep," he repeated wearily, his throat raw from crying and cold. He lit another smoke, his fingers aching icicles. It didn't feel right to just leave the animal here to rot, but he couldn't bury it; winter had turned the ground to rock. He'd have to load the body in the truck, he decided, and take it with him. Give it some kind of funeral rites later, maybe, fruity as that sounded.

Besides, he rationalized, he'd love to know what exactly it was, and bringing the body along was the best way to find out, right?

He needed to get gloves from the truck before his fingers snapped off in the cold. He had some rope and tarp in a box behind the cab, along with his pricey little package of pills, protected by a litter of rusty fishhooks and long-unused lures.

Adler was turning from the body back toward the truck when he heard that awful music start up again, an eerie chord that locked his every muscle. It began in his bones, but climbed into his ears quicker than before, becoming a melancholy keen that raised every hair on his body. Adler broke the spell it threw over him just enough to turn toward the sound.

Its source stood between him and the truck, its triangular head hung low, its eyes blazing at him, searing into him, concentrating every ray of reflected starlight into two sloe-shaped flames.

White-Out

That scream-song hadn't been a death cry. The creature he'd hit was dead, yes, but it had probably died on impact. It had been a cry of mourning, probably for a slain mate. Or a cub.

Or a cry of revenge against the thing that, out of nowhere, struck that cub down.

The thought came from nowhere, or from those flaming eyes. Either way, it seized him with its certainty.

This one looked bigger than the first, but maybe that was just the effect of its raised hackles and its bared teeth, just as blood-dark as those of its dead mate. Or the effect of Adler's terror.

Adler's eyes were fixed on its twin fires, and then, they were gone. Could an animal really move that fast? His brain barely registered the tracer-arc left by its flung body, the quick gleam of starlight on its claws and teeth as it fell on him. It was an avalanche, compacted into a package of muscle and fur, bearing him to the ground.

Adler opened his mouth to scream. Instead of sound, he was surprised to find it full of viscous heat that sprayed out, spattering the berry-littered snow.

Its triangular head hammered down, and an array of incurving teeth dug into his throat. The force of its attack tamped him down into the reddening bank, where his thrashing swept angels into the speckled snow. His arms ineffectually battered its sides, folding over its back in a convulsive embrace.

As his life fled his torn throat, seeping out through the snow and flooding the animal's mouth, Adler held it close, closer than he'd ever held Sharyl or any other lover, closer than he'd ever been held. He was amazed at the silky softness of its white fur, despite the patches made tacky by his blood.

Along with the blood, his fear gushed out. Adler lay on his back, a warmly vibrating weight pressing his chest. His face upturned, he saw the white-laden trees leaning in, ready to whisper to him, and the stars winked at him knowingly.

A few lazy flakes of snow drifted down. He marveled at how powdery dry they looked until they landed wetly on his face. He wondered, with his body opened up in all that cold, why he felt so warm, and why the sky had finally decided to wear the whiteness of the snow.

The snow, on the other hand, had donned a spreading coat of mottled red, as had the creature that had arisen from it. Its long tongue snaked quickly back and forth, lapping the gradually slowing rush of blood from his throat. Its jaws dripped with rivulets and gobbets of him, and the pallid smear of his fading face reflected back to him in the brightness of its beautiful eyes. Mother's eyes, they surely were, and lover's eyes, lit with suffering and wisdom, neither human nor animal.

The thinning tissue of his consciousness shifted and shredded as easily as his flesh. Her jaws worked lower, teeth tearing the flesh over his clavicle and into his ribs, which rose whitely from their bed of muscle and meat.

She wasn't merely feasting. She opened him up with resolute efficiency; her teeth unzipped his body as expertly as her eyes penetrated his mind. She took his ability to feel his body, with its pervasive pain, and she took his thoughts, too; he realized this when her matted, reddened muzzle rose, breath steaming in a moment of respite, and she breathed, with terrible clarity, "For my little one."

Then her head moved lower once more, tearing through his navel, shearing down to his pubic bone.

Adler's last impression was of the deliberate care with which she dug out his guts, her sharp teeth not puncturing the organs, lifting them out as gently as a mother wolf might lift her cubs. Her head sunk and rose, sunk and rose, drawing out his intestines and laying them in steaming heaps in the snow. Those organs seemed to Adler interminably long, for by the time she had tugged the last of them from their cavity, his consciousness was gone.

White-Out

Indifferent to his absence, she continued her work on his lush husk. By the time his opened corpse and discarded organs had ceased to steam and his pooled blood ceased to melt the snow, congealing instead into red-brown soft-pack, she had gutted him to her satisfaction.

She moved to her fallen cub next, her eyes of fire shedding hot tears, sluicing thin trails through her gore-smeared face. She bathed his face with her tongue, lapped his eyes closed, let her blood-pink tears wash his coat. Then, with the greatest tenderness and with surgical precision, slit him from chin to groin and stripped off his precious white hide.

This labor of grief complete, she paused, tonguing clotted matter from her jaws, from her face, from her claw-tipped paws, from her long, graceful limbs. She basked in the sensation, as though afraid to forget how this quick, sleek form felt.

Finally, she was ready for the task at hand, to drape herself in the drunken primate's remains.

She wriggled, hindquarters first, down into the flesh-and-bone envelope she had hollowed from his trunk. Just as the blood had slaked her hunger, the humid warmth of this meat-cave quickly numbed the cold burn of her rage, the agony of her loss.

The languor of burrowing in a strange body washed over her. She tucked her limbs below, curled her long tail beside her huddled body.

Eyes heavy-lidded, heart rate slowing, lassitude filling her, she let pure instinct guide her teeth and tongue as they worked to close the mouth of her meat shelter. Dead flesh knit as her teeth stitched and her saliva sealed. Her ministrations worked their magic, and the man's rent flesh was soldered, sealing her, dreaming powerfully, in the womb of what he had been.

The body stopped its cooling, early stirrings of its entropy cancelled. Lying for an undisclosed span in the painted snow, it did not fall stiff, did not grow hoary with frost.

Eventually, she opened the man's eyes and rose to his two clumsy feet. She had hoped not to walk in human skin again for a long, long time. But she had lost her child, and her nerves, which were the timeless wisdom of her ancestors, told her she needed these weak primate eyes to find the means to birth a new one.

Driven by this knowledge, she found the shovel that the dead man's mind told her was kept in the bed of his truck, and she used it to heap snow across the blood-spattered scene. Stripped of its hide, her cub's body was already collapsing upon itself. She knew too well that soon there would be little left to mark his passing, aside from the pelt she carried in her thick human hands.

She wrapped the dead man's offal and other remains in a garbage bag, also taken from the truck bed. Then she breathed in the night, trying to discern the details she needed through his crude nose, trying to filter out the odorous fugue of his flesh.

Finding the bright scent-signs she needed, she walked off through the woods, toward the clustered scents and sounds of the town to the north.

Stowaway

by P. R. O'Leary

On the ground floor, 192 stories down, Stig covered his head and face with the rainsuit hood and walked out into the street. The driving rain and heavy smog obscured his view, so the smell hit him first. He could never get used to it. Take every bad smell that comes out of a person's body, multiply it by a billion, and sprinkle some landfills and industrial waste on top. That was the smell of the city. It was almost visible.

Even through the rain and smog and smell, Stig could see that the street was crowded with people, packed end-to-end as usual, bodies moving in every direction, pushing and jostling each other for space. Cars had long since become impractical, and the public Tubes were always out of commission, so they had no choice but to walk, especially in this area, characterized by people who had no other means besides their own two legs—and sometimes not even that.

Stig pushed through the crowd as the rain pounded the top of his head. There was no telling what anyone looked like below their rainsuits. People were making every effort to cover their skin, including him.

Most of Stig's rainsuit had eroded down to the red warning layer, and in some places, the rain had eaten all the way through. His hands, arms, back, and face were covered in white scars where the water had seared his flesh. Stig couldn't afford to patch the rainsuit anymore; good acid-blocking material was out of his price range. The adequate kind was, too.

If you caught a look at Stig's face, you would instantly be able to tell what caste of society he belonged to. Those white scars, starting on his hairless scalp and running down his face like tears, showed that he couldn't protect himself from the rain. The black pupils in the center of red, smog-damaged eyes showed that he couldn't afford eye-whitening. The dirt and grease in the lines of his face spoke of a hard life without access to more than the standard ration of dirty water.

But at least he wasn't a Faceless, one of those who couldn't even afford what Stig had. They lived on the streets, faces scarred into obscurity from exposure, lips and eyes gone, mouths permanently open, always wanting.

The thought that he still had a face almost made Stig smile. He forced his perpetual grimace into a smirk, but still looked like he was ready to kill someone. That look was probably the only thing Stig had going for him, a look that said, "Don't mess with me. I may be covered in rain-scars but that won't stop this towering beast, full of 40 years of rage, from crushing you to death with his massive hands."

That look was what kept him safe, and it was also what earned him his job. The job and the silver at the end were the only things that could convince him to brave the streets.

The streets had more people on them every day. The population was exploding; rural areas turned into towns; towns turned into cities; cities built inward, and when there was no room, everything began to build up toward the sky. After that, to save even more space, things started getting smaller: Cube housing, rations, personal space. With no end in sight, governments began to look elsewhere for places where humanity could live.

Every few weeks, a ship was sent out into space with a frozen crew on board, aimed at some likely candidate planet in a faraway galaxy, like Sagittarius, Andromeda, or Ursa Minor. But those journeys took centuries; they weren't going to help anyone alive today.

More importantly, they were starting to take advantage of Mars, which was being terraformed. It now had oxygen, water, plants, animals, farms, and miles of open space. Ships containing colonists and supplies were being sent there monthly. Stig would have loved to get a ticket on one of those ships, but they were only for the rich, and even they had to give up all of their Earthly possessions to raise the money to buy one.

So Stig was stuck where congestion, famine, and pollution reigned, where buildings were cramped honeycombs and the sky was always covered in dark, smelly clouds that poured out horrible, stinging rain.

Stig only had to walk one kilometer to get to work, but that still took an entire hour of pushing, glaring, and constantly readjusting his rainsuit so it covered his most sensitive areas. He reached Plastique just before his shift started.

In this part of town, every business needed some muscle around, especially a strip club. Stig's job was to stand by the door, thankfully out of the rain, and make sure the customers didn't get out of hand. In return, he got a measly paycheck and the opportunity to watch the ladies do their dances onstage.

It wasn't as good as you might think. There was only so long that he could look at a naked woman and wonder if these white lines on her body were rain-scars, drugged veins, the remnants of some back-alley surgery, or just good old-fashioned stretch marks.

This was his last shift. Stig just needed to get to the end and collect his pay from the boss. That last fistful of grimy silver bills would put him over the top, and with it, Stig just might be able to get off of this stinking planet for good.

First, he needed to steel himself for one last 12-hour shift, a shift with no shortage of distractions. An old man, older than Stig's father would have been if he were still alive, tried to climb on the stage and mount a woman. The man's body was light and frail like a bag of sticks, but he screamed, cursed, and tried to scratch as Stig tossed him out into the street. Stig didn't feel bad about throwing him out.

The one incident that did bother him, and something that happened far too often, was one of the Faceless trying to force his way into the club. At least, Stig thought it was a "he."

It was a pale, scarred body covered in discarded rags, topped with a face like a melted candle. A black hole in the middle and two pools of what was left of eyes stared at him. Stig had to push it out and stand by the door, blocking the poor creature from the warm and dry sanctuary he desperately needed. Eventually, the thing moved on.

But that was the last Faceless he would subject to the pain of exposure just to get his hands on some silver. When the boss paid him out of the locked safe in the back room, Stig said goodbye and left, just like it was any other day. But in his mind he was also saying, "Good riddance."

♦

The idea first formed a year earlier, when Stig saved someone's life. Well, "saved" was a strong word, but he did stop the guy from getting stabbed. It was nothing unusual, just an altercation at the club, possibly over a table or a drink or a woman. A knife was drawn, so Stig jumped in, broke it up, and threw out the offender. All in a day's work.

The man he saved, Haggal Strom, bought him a drink later, as thanks. They got to talking, and it turned out that Haggal worked as a security guard at the airfield, the facility at the edge of the city that shot off rockets.

Was it then that the idea entered Stig's head? Maybe. He dreamed of Mars soon after, and slowly, the idea germinated into a real plan.

Over the next few months, Stig kept in contact with Haggal. He asked about Haggal's job, and about the airfield and the shuttle flights. He plied him for information, carefully, so Haggal wouldn't know what Stig's true motives were.

They had an easygoing rapport, but they weren't quite friends, more like comrades who had drawn pretty much the same lot in life and respected one another for dealing with it. That respect was what Stig hoped would make Haggal accept his bargain.

When Stig felt like he had enough information and wasn't just shooting for the moon, he finally asked Haggal: "Can you get me on a shuttle to Mars?"

Stig knew it was crazy. Even if he got on the shuttle unnoticed, he would have to find a way to survive undetected for two months before landing, and then somehow make it off the shuttle and past the authorities at the check-in.

But after that, Stig would be free. He could go find a nice private corner of the planet, build a shelter, and live off the land. He knew how. He was doing research from old books and magazines from the digital archives that showed the tools and the tricks. Stig hadn't seen a tree since he was a child, but he know if he could get out there in the wild, green open, then he could do it. And if not, then at least he would die a happy man in fresh air and sunlight.

Haggal took some convincing, but Stig knew he understood. In the end, all Stig had to do was offer up all his worldly possessions, his Cube, and the large sum of silver that he had just finished saving.

It was time to find Haggal and plan his trip to Mars.

◆

They met at the usual place: the back of the Bolted Arm, a somewhat less shady bar than most. The place was packed, as usual. The patrons were not spending enough money to earn personal space, so there were no tables. It was standing room only, but Haggal and Stig knew a corner that featured a small alcove. If they glared enough at people—Haggal could look almost as intimidating as Stig—the occupants would vacate and leave a good three square feet of space where Stig and Haggal could stand, drink and talk.

This time, though, Stig didn't buy a drink. He couldn't afford it; all his money was going directly to Haggal. It made Stig feel lighter somehow, as if he was no longer tethered to his Cube and his possessions. Once the deal was done, all Stig would own was the clothes he was wearing, including the worthless rainsuit.

Haggal was already in the bar, leaning up against the corner, cocky as ever. He was still wearing his work uniform: a padded blue outfit that made his already bulky frame even more bulky, big black boots, and a black thing on his head that was half hat, half helmet. Bits of stringy hair stuck out from under it, and a gray, curly beard and mustache were sprouting from his face. He was pushing 50 but looked like he could still move quickly.

In the past few weeks, Haggal had been hard to read. When Stig had first mentioned the plan, Haggal seemed trustworthy and practical, but as the moment drew closer, he seemed a bit off. Maybe Stig's nervousness was clouding his thinking, but Haggal always seemed to avoid eye contact when speaking and was evasive about details.

As Stig walked up to him in their corner, shoving through the mass of fleshy drinkers, he caught a glimpse of Haggal. Was the man pensive? Nervous? Before Stig could draw any conclusions, Haggal noticed him coming and was suddenly all smiles.

"Hey, Stig! How's it going, man?" He tipped his plastic cup toward him.

"Fine, Haggal." Stig tried to catch him off guard. "But cut the crap. I have your money; I just finished collecting it today. We need to go over the details of my trip."

Haggal's smile shrank, but didn't drop. "Okay, okay. I was just asking how you were, man. Don't freak out. Anyway, I've been figuring out the details for a month now."

Stig couldn't tell if Haagal was being genuine or not. For a second, he thought about giving up on this crazy idea, but then he remembered the Faceless he shoved out of the club earlier, and its eyes, or lack thereof. The molten face had shown nothing but need. Eventually, everyone on Earth would become Faceless.

"Okay," Stig said. "Let's hear these details."

The plan was simple. There was a launch scheduled in a week, and Haggal would be working during the correct shift. Stig would enter the airbase through a specified delivery gate at a specified time and walk quickly but casually to the second building on the left. He would take the gray door, walk down the hallway, and enter the last door on the right, which would be ajar. The door would lock behind him automatically.

In that room, there were stacks of metal cases scheduled to be loaded onto the shuttle. There would be one extra that Haggal had managed to sneak onto the manifest, and it would be empty. It was numbered 146-53a. Stig would climb in, close the lid, wait 14 hours, and hang on for the ride of his life. If he survived the takeoff and two months of space travel—which was questionable—he would make it to Mars.

After Stig got on the shuttle and the shuttle took off, Haggal would have earned his payment. If the plan worked, they would never see each other again. On the other hand, if it didn't work, Stig would go to jail. And if you thought normal public places were overcrowded, you should have seen the prisons.

Haggal would get paid up front, so it worked out for him either way. Stig could only trust in the man's human decency and hope that he was telling the truth.

Stig spent the next few agonizingly slow days repeating the plan in his head.

Delivery Gate. 1:15 a.m. Second building on the left. Gray door. Hallway. Last door on the right. Metal Case. 146-53a.

Gate. 1:15. Building. Gray door. Right. 146-53a.

146-53a.
146-53a.
146-53a.

◆

Haggal got his payment the day before the launch. It was anticlimactic; Stig literally just dropped off the payment, a bound pile of silver the size of a loaf of bread, at Haagel's Cube. Stig's Cube was transferred over to Haggal at the building's office. He gave Haggal his entry bracelet, and that was that. Stig felt no sense of loss.

He spent that night walking around the fenced-off perimeter of the airfield. Nighttime lightened the load of people on the street, but not by much, so it still took a while to get there.

Luckily, it was only drizzling, and the rainsuit had enough life left in it to keep Stig dry. Maybe it was an omen, or maybe the Earth knew it was Stig's last night here and was trying to entice him to stay. But lessening the relentless acid downpour that had dropped on Stig's head nearly every day of his life was too little, too late.

Stig arrived at the delivery gate two hours before schedule and found a safe place to wait, leaning against a building with a good view of his target. It was a small gate in a chain-link fence, and the whole thing was topped with barbwire. Behind it, he could see the complex: a mass of buildings huddled together. The space between the buildings, although narrow, was empty.

Not a single person was behind the gate. Stig couldn't see why the gate would be unlocked, but he waited until his watch said 1:14am and then walked toward it. Squeezing through the unending crowd, Stig knew this would be the first test of Haggal's trustworthiness.

One minute later, Stig got through the stream of people and reached the gate, pushing it open without hesitation. It gave easily. He let it fall back into place and kept moving as quickly and casually as possible before the crowd could follow him in.

For a moment, the sensation of open space around him was overwhelming. It had been a long time since Stig had been out in the open. Usually, there were people pushing him from all sides, or too-close walls limiting his movements, or too-short ceilings holding him down. He fought the urge to stop and instead just reached out his arms and tried to stretch his body in all directions while he kept moving.

There still weren't any people in the complex, which was a good sign, and there was a gray door on the second building on the left, which was an even better sign.

Stig walked right up and pulled it open. Straight ahead was a long hallway lit by stark bright lights on the ceiling. The walls were unadorned, and everything was rimmed in industrial metal and plastic. There were several doors along either side.

Stig's eyes searched quickly for the last one on the right. Was it closed? He couldn't tell. He started walking toward it as quickly and silently as his bulky body would allow.

His breathing was so loud that anyone in the building would have been able to hear him. Halfway down the hallway, he heard a click behind him as one of the doors opened up. Stig froze for a split second and then continued walking as casually as possible. He had no choice but to look like he belonged there. He just kept moving, without running or turning. There was silence for a few seconds, then a click as the door behind him closed. Nothing else.

Stig realized he wasn't breathing and rectified that. He could see the last door on the right now. Yes! It was open, barely. The door was resting against the frame, and a good tap would send it closed and probably locked. Stig's big, clumsy hands were shaking as he opened it, and he almost knocked it shut. But he managed to open it, jump into the completely dark room, and close the door behind him. He heard the door lock and reached for the handle to check, but there wasn't one.

He couldn't see a thing in the blackness, so he started feeling for the knob or a light switch with his hands. Nothing. Stig was stuck in darkness, and he didn't even know if he was in the right room. Even if he was, he somehow had to find a case with a very specific number on it and climb inside.

Stig had lots of time, so he tried to relax, slowing his breathing and heart rate. No use getting panicked. He rationalized that he was safe in there until it was closer to launch time. He just needed to let his eyes adjust, then find the case.

It took a bit longer than Stig would have liked, but soon he could see shapes, specifically large rectangular boxes stacked on top of one another. There were about 40 in this room. He also saw a dark square on the back wall, probably some sort of door for loading and unloading the boxes.

Stig walked slowly toward the closest case and stared at it. After what felt like hours, he started to see big, dark text on the front of it. Rubbing his fingers over the markings, he could feel where they were painted or burned on. Numbers and letters. 132-19c. That was good. Not the right number, but at least now he now knew how to find it.

He began checking each case, running his hands over their covers, climbing carefully over them in order to remain quiet, and only moving those he had to.

It wasn't long before he found it, in the third stack from the end of the leftmost row. The one on the top was clearly labeled 146-53a. Stig stared at it to be sure, running his hand along the numbers. Yes! It was definitely the right one.

Stig snapped the magnetic latch open. It looked empty inside, just a metal case padded with foam. He probed the interior with his arm to verify that it was. He closed it again, and the magnetic latch caught automatically. Perfect. He was so happy he almost kissed it.

He popped it open again, squeezed himself down inside, and closed the lid behind him. It was cramped, and after a few minutes, it started to hurt, but Stig was too excited to care. Besides, he didn't want to risk waiting outside the case. The next time Stig came out, he would be on his way to Mars. He just hoped he would be alive when it happened.

♦

Inside the case, it was completely black. Stig's nose was pressed up against his forearm, but he still couldn't see his watch, so without knowing exactly how long to wait, he concentrated on other things. Shifting his body in the tight space, a millimeter at a time, he eventually found a position where the pressure was off of his tender bits and his joints were not twisted at such awkward angles.

His hand rested against the lid. He could feel some engravings in the corner and traced them with his fingertips. The writing was too tiny to feel the individual letters, but Stig spent some time imagining what the words were. He imagined that this case was his coffin and the writing was his epitaph: "Here lies Stig Vurlock. / He tried to make it to Mars, but instead / he perished in flight and lies here, dead."

Eventually, that grew tiresome, so without anything in the physical space to occupy him, Stig turned to his other senses. His ears strained for sounds outside the case and outside the room. Once in a while, he heard distant noises like footsteps and the opening and closing of a door, but nothing nearby. The wait was interminable, and even though his positioning was fairly solid, he had a huge urge to open up the case to stand, stretch, and look at his watch.

Then, there was the loud sound of a power source turning on, an engine or motor or battery, and the deep rumble of something moving nearby. Maybe it was a vehicle outside? Or the loading door? Before Stig could determine what it was, the case began jostling slightly, then more forcefully as the sound of pneumatics filled his ears. The case was being moved!

It wasn't so bad. Stig could brace himself so the jostling barely caused any discomfort, but suddenly, the world spun and gravity twisted as the case was violently lifted, and based on how it felt, tumbled down the side of a mountain.

Stig flexed every muscle in his body to try to fill up the space and keep from bouncing around, but it was too much and the movements were too unpredictable. He didn't know what to prepare for next. His shoulders banged painfully against the sides. His fingers bent while trying to hold his body still. His head hit the top (or bottom or side) of the case, causing lumps and maybe even bleeding.

Then it stopped and there was only a steady hum. Was it from inside Stig's head? A few more bumps jostled him again, like aftershocks, and then all was still and silent.

Nothing.

Stig waited, fearful of more. He hoped he was in the ship, but there was no way to find out. It was too dangerous to open the case, so he just stuck to the plan and waited. The throbbing pain all over his body felt like a physical presence in the box with him. Eventually, he fought it off.

Maybe he dozed, maybe not. It was hard to tell. There was silence for a long time and then, without warning, a sudden roar, a sound so loud that for a second, Stig thought his head was exploding. And when he thought he was hearing the loudest sound in the world, it just kept getting louder and wouldn't stop. The roar grew and grew.

Stig couldn't move his hands to cover his ears, so he pushed one side of his head against the wall of the case, but that didn't help. Then there was a horrible weight, something pushing him down into the ground. The roar grew louder and the pushing became more and more intense.

Everything was being driven down into the ground. He couldn't move his body, couldn't even breathe. His lungs would not work. His face was pressed into the bottom of the case, and all of his blood felt like it was trying to push out of his eyeballs. White flashes of light began appearing everywhere and the last thing he thought before passing out was that they looked like stars.

♦

Stig awoke floating in utter silence. He was no longer pressed into the ground, and instead felt light and airy like the gas inside a balloon. Then there was a click and his body regained weight, falling back into its original cramped position.

Stig didn't know how injured he was. All of his bones felt broken and his organs felt mushy, but at least he was alive. He tentatively moved parts of his body. Fingers and toes. Arms, legs, neck. Eyelids. Everything was painful but in working order.

There was no sound outside the case, but Stig waited a few minutes just to be sure. Was it really this quiet, or did his ears just stop working? Either way, he needed to get outside of these confines. Luckily, he was still able to reach the latch and squeeze the contacts together. The magnetic clasp let go, allowing him to push open the lid.

Bright light streamed in, blinding him, but with it came fresh air and much needed space. Stig kept his eyes closed and stood up. His body stretched out luxuriously, and no part of it fell off. It was wobbly, but at least in one piece.

Slowly opening his eyes, he could see that he was in a small room filled with cases. It wasn't really a room, though, more like a chamber bound by curved metal beams. There was one door leading out, a hatch with a white wheel in the center instead of a doorknob. There were about a dozen cases on the floor, each strapped down with a large black band attached to bolts in the floor. Stig was in the middle of them. Otherwise, the room was empty.

He stepped carefully out of the case. The artificial gravity was different from what Stig was used to. He felt slightly lighter. He was in space. Space! The plan was working so far. Haggal had come through, and Stig was now on his way to Mars.

The next phase was survival. He needed to find a store of food and water, as well as a place to hide while he made the trip. He needed to do it quickly, since he was unsure how many people were going to be walking around the ship.

Stig started climbing over the cases and opening them. The first contained some sort of electronic device, a black pane with buttons and a video screen. He closed it quickly. The second contained a pile of thick white fabric. Stig dug his hand through but found nothing. The third case contained exactly what he was looking for.

It was stacked full of high-energy food packs, protein bars, and vitamin powder—everything he needed except water. If he could steal a small amount of it each day, even every few days, he would be in great shape. He took two handfuls of sustenance and put them in his pockets.

The rest of the cases yielded no water. Stig had to risk leaving the room to find something to drink. Cautiously, he pressed his ear against the cold metal of the door and heard nothing but the quiet hum of the ship. He turned the wheel carefully and opened it.

Banks of computers covered the walls. Recessed into them were six large glass coffins, standing upright from floor to ceiling. Each one held a naked human being, with tubes in their mouths and nostrils, suspended in a blue liquid. Numbers and graphs drifted across screens below them showing heart rate, pulse, and blood pressure. There were nameplates above the vessels: Dr. Bridgett Fontaine, Dr. Mobeus Heimlitz, Captain Greg Reynolds.

Stig's mouth dropped open. A frozen crew? For a two-month-long voyage? What about the passengers? He went to a computer terminal, frantically pressing buttons and touching the screen, but didn't know the correct commands and got no information. Desperately, he looked around the room for anything that would give the ship's destination, anything that said, "Mars."

Then he remembered the case and the small writing on the inside, the words that occupied him for his long wait before launch time. He ran back into the room and found the case, the one he so willingly locked himself into: Case 146-53a.

Stig opened the lid, shaking. The markings were there, small black letters etched into the corner: "CONTENTS: 1 month solid rations, 6-member crew. DESTINATION: Planet 15025, System H-154, Andromeda."

Healer

by Jean Davis

Jillian breathed deep through her nose and focused on the young man on the hospital bed beside her. His breathing remained troubled, even after the two-hour healing session she'd just performed. Doctors and nurses hovered in the hallway, poking in their heads from time to time to check on her progress. The pleading eyes of the man's wife on the other side of the bed, along with the photo of their two children on the bedside table, wouldn't allow her to give up.

She took a few moments to focus on the room, giving her body time to regroup. The remaining session would drain her, but she was so close with Mike that she didn't dare stop now. He needed her.

Someone always did. The next patients on her list would have to hold on another day.

The television was silent, but photos of missing children still appeared behind the newscaster. Jillian secretly wished someone would steal her away. To be free of obligation, guilt and constant fatigue … she sighed.

She again rested her hand on her patient's cool, clammy arm, re-forming the lifeline that linked them together. Jillian summoned the gift within her.

A tingle rose in her chest, building, then flowing upward into her shoulders. It shot down her left arm and swelled in her hand. There, the tingle coalesced until it gathered heat.

Jillian let go of her body, knowing it would remain in the chair as if she were asleep, waiting for her return. Her awareness seeped through the palm of her hand and into the arm of the man on the bed.

His heartbeat became hers as she traveled along his arm, winding, twisting her way toward his chest. Their heartbeat grew louder, accompanied by the droning of rushing blood.

Somewhere in the room, people were talking—probably the attending doctor, checking in again. The sound reminded Jillian of when she was younger, listening to her mother chat with her friends in distant, muffled voices while she and the other children played underwater tag in the neighbor's pool. Those pleasant, lazy days were long gone.

Spreading herself through the body, she sought out the black shadows of illness and burned them away with her heat. When all the shadows had been vanquished elsewhere, she focused on the stubborn ones lingering in the lungs.

She knew she was making progress when the body insisted that its name was Mike. He hadn't been aware enough the last few times to put up any internal fight. Now, he attempted to push her away.

She pressed her thoughts on his defensive force. "I'm trying to help."

Sometimes bodies were receptive to her presence, talking with her and allowing her to control their muscles and functions as she needed, but most men didn't seem to like her female presence. Perhaps it was too foreign to them.

Mike fought, using his precious energy to oppose her rather than resting. Muscles bunched up, squeezing and shifting, escaping her calming control and dividing her focus.

Jillian didn't want to find out what would happen if a patient died while they were both entangled in a healing trance. Would she die when her lifeline collapsed, or become a passenger, stuck in someone else's body? If he got too aggravated, she'd have to abort her mission or risk finding out.

The shadows taunted her, dark and boiling with malignant energy. These were the times Jillian wished she had weapons other than willpower and heat, but swords or handguns couldn't follow her into a patient's body, and medicine had failed. This was a war she had to fight alone.

Jillian gathered her being into a cloud that rivaled the size and mass of the shadows. Heat pulsated and grew, glowing a deep red at the edges of her hazy vision. Energy crackled within her.

For a moment, she swore she saw white eyes glaring at her from within the shadows, then they were gone, and like the other times her imagination had played the same trick on her, a chill ran through her being, disrupting her focus.

The shadows formed a wall. The line of war had been established.

Jillian let her heat build until her exit path began to tremble. If she let go of the path, she'd have no way to retreat back to her own body. She considered calling off her efforts for the day and coming back tomorrow recharged, but the thought of Mike dying while she rested peacefully goaded her onward.

The healing heat rose until she could hold it no longer. She hurled it at the shadows. They absorbed the heat and extinguished its faint, nebulous glow. Shaking with exhaustion, Jillian backed away.

Instead of growing and coming after her as she feared, the shadows began to pulse. They faded from black to a deep gray, then grew lighter and lighter until they dissipated entirely.

Relief washed over her as she drifted away. Unable to muster any more energy of her own, she let the faint lifeline return her to her own body.

Jillian gasped as her awareness synchronized with the breathing of her own lungs and beating of her own heart. She squeezed her eyes shut against the bright hospital lights, dropped her head into her hands, and wished nothing more than to be in her bed at the hotel across the street.

"You did it! Just look at him, he looks better already," an exuberant voice informed her. Arms wrapped around Jillian's shoulders and squeezed her tightly. "I can't thank you enough."

"It's okay, really." Jillian resisted the urge to push Mike's wife away. She needed space. She needed sleep. Mike's wife clutched his limp hand while beaming at her as if she'd just performed a miracle.

"Your gift is precious. Don't pay any attention to the doubters. People can't just jump up from terminal cancer and go about their lives as if they'd suffered nothing more than a mild headache. True healing takes time, and you make that time possible." She reached out and took Jillian's hand, forming a link between the three of them. "I would be happy to stand by your side and tell the world how wrong they are."

"That's not necessary." Jillian mustered a weak smile. "I just want to help where I can, and remember, you signed the contract."

"I know, but you could help so many more people if they truly understood."

Jillian slipped her hand from the woman's loose grasp. "This hospital, these doctors, they support me well enough. I'm not looking for fame."

Her energy wasn't infinite. She was only one person and she could only do so much. People wouldn't understand that any more than the fact that she only could offer aid in healing, not instant recovery.

She'd had enough of public ridicule, along with the dueling stacks of hate mail and desperate pleas for her help. That was why she worked out of a hotel, hiding behind a wall of confidentiality contracts.

Dr. Kellar entered the room and went directly to Mike's side. He checked Mike's breathing and pulse, then turned to smile at Jillian.

"We'll have to run tests, of course, but from what I can see here, his condition has vastly improved. Thank you, Ms. Baare."

Jillian nodded.

"Would you like someone to take you to your room?"

"That would be wonderful, thank you." As tired as she was, the walk to her hotel room across the street seemed like a trip to another country.

Dr. Kellar left, and moments later, an attendant came in, pushing a wheelchair. He wheeled it over to where Jillian sat.

"Do you need help?"

She shook her head. Her hands and arms trembled as she grabbed the arms of the wheelchair and swung herself into it. She dropped into the seat with an unceremonious thump.

Mike's wife hovered over him, still holding his hand and grinning from ear to ear as tears slipped down her cheeks. She met Jillian's gaze.

"Thank you. I wish there were more I could say."

"I wish there were more I could do."

"I wouldn't ask it of you, even if you could. You're exhausted. Go, rest." She offered her benediction with a smile and shooing motion.

Jillian nodded to the attendant, who pushed her out of the room and down the hall to the elevator.

"You did a good thing in there," he said.

"Thanks."

They always had kind words for her after the fact. It was the begging and pleading beforehand that rubbed her nerves raw. Then again, her nerves were raw after a healing session, too. Couldn't she just teleport to her room so she didn't have to talk to anyone else? That would be a handy gift to have.

Jillian realized the attendant wasn't heading for the hotel. "Where are we going?"

"The cafeteria. Last time I helped you, you made me promise to take you there before we returned to the hotel. You told me not to take 'no' for an answer because you needed to eat. Excuse me for saying so, but you look three times worse today. You're going to eat something."

She couldn't help but smile. The staff did take good care of her, despite the fact that she tended to attract unwelcome attention from reporters and naysayers, no matter how many aliases she used or how low a profile she kept.

"Thank you."

After devouring a ham and cheese sandwich without tasting a bite of it, Jillian sat back, and the attendant resumed their trip back to the hotel.

With her stomach full, her eyes began to sag. The bright overhead lights seemed to blink on and off. Waking glimpses of white hallways lined with multicolored stripes informed her that she was approaching the tunnel under the busy street that connected the hospital and the hotel.

The whirring of the wheels changed tones as they entered the tunnel, echoing off the tile walls. A mother scolded a child in the distance. A conversation about an ailing grandmother and who was covering the insurance deductible grew in volume and then faded away.

She pried her head off her shoulder when her chair came to a halt.

"Ms. Baare can't be bothered right now," the attendant said. "No. She doesn't do interviews. Please excuse us."

The chair set off again. The rhythmic steps of the attendant began lulling her to sleep, but the ding of the elevator brought her around again. Seconds later, the attendant delivered Jillian to her hotel room door.

A woman in scrubs approached them. "I'll take her from here."

"I'll be fine," said Jillian.

"Oh, nonsense. It's plain to see how tired you are. You work so hard here; let me help you."

The woman waved the attendant off. Jillian fumbled in her pants pocket for the keycard. The woman took it from her and slid it into the lock. The door clicked.

Healer

"Now, let's get you into bed." She rolled the wheelchair into the room.

Jillian tried to see the name on the ID card hanging around the woman's neck. Using their names usually made them feel acknowledged so they'd leave her alone. The woman kept moving, adjusting the chair alongside the bed, then helped Jillian to her feet.

She gave up trying to be polite and snapped, "I'm fine now, really."

The woman left her side and went to the door. The lights went out. The lock clicked shut.

Jillian let herself relax and sank back onto the bed. Just as she was drifting off to sleep, the door opened and the lights came back on.

"Who's there?"

"Stay where you are."

The woman was standing in the doorway with a young child in her arms. She rushed to the bed and placed the girl next to Jillian, then pulled a gun from the back of her waistband.

"Heal her."

Sweat broke out on Jillian's brow, and her hands grew clammy. She'd seen many horrible diseases in her years as a healer, but none of them struck her as deeply as the sight of the bloody two-year-old wearing a yellow sundress, with a bullet hole in her abdomen.

"I can't."

"Don't lie to me. That man confirmed who you were in the tunnel, so I know you can. You just don't want to." She leveled the gun at Jillian. "How about now?"

"I'm sorry." She looked down at the pale face of the little girl and felt within herself, checking her energy. It wasn't enough; she'd drained too much on Mike. It would be another full day before she would be ready to face her waiting list. "Send her across the street. The doctors can fix her."

"I can't. You do it."

"Why would you wait here for me when there's a hospital right there? What kind of mother are you?"

"You don't understand!" The woman's shrill voice rose to a wail. "If you don't save her, she'll die! My baby will die!"

"Keep your voice down."

The last thing Jillian needed was more attention, for the media to grab onto the story and drag her through the mud again, bringing another host of desperate people to her door. She'd have to find a new hospital in a new city. A whole new raft of contracts and agreements floated before her eyes, blurring the view of the girl bleeding on her bed.

The mother waved the gun at her, moving closer.

"I don't care what it costs. You will heal my daughter. Now."

"Please, put that away. I'll do what I can for her, but you'll have to take her to the hospital as soon as I'm done. I won't be able to do more than stabilize her."

"I can't go to the hospital."

"Of course you can. If you don't have money, they'll work with you. They're not heartless."

"They'll find out and they'll take Emily from me. I can't let them do that; I can't."

Jillian ignored the woman's voice and sunk deep into herself. The only way to get the gun out of her face was to help Emily. She took the girl's hand and melted inward, leaving Emily's mother behind.

The room dimmed, and her vision took on a red tinge. The familiar tingle within her grew, swelling until it pushed her into the little girl's body.

Emily's pulse was faint. The shadows had a firm hold on her young body, and pitch black clouds surrounded the bullet hole. Grayness pulsated everywhere Jillian looked. There was so much to fix, so many shadows.

The distant muffled voice of the woman rose higher. Jillian

faltered. She began to wonder about the safety of the body she'd left behind. Would the woman shoot her, thinking she'd fainted? She'd had no time to explain the process.

Determined to at least make an honest effort, Jillian concentrated her heat on the vital organs. The shadows surrounding the girl's heart ebbed.

Jillian pulled back into her own body. "I've done all I can. You need to get her to the hospital now." Her voice trembled with exhaustion.

"I won't let them take my baby away."

Emily's mother leveled her gun at Jillian. She held up her hands as if skin and bone could shield her from a bullet.

"I wish I could do more. I'm very sorry, but I really need to rest now."

"No."

"Lady, you won't have a baby to lose if you don't get her to the hospital immediately."

"I'll kill you if you don't heal her."

"A lot of good that will do; your daughter and I will both be dead."

"I don't have much choice. You know my secret."

"Look, whatever your secret is, you know mine too. Your daughter will die if you don't go. Please."

"They'll find out she isn't mine." The woman fired the gun.

Jillian's heart forgot how to beat. She screamed. The room dimmed and then got brighter again. Bile rose in her throat. She realized she wasn't hurt, but she still felt the urge to throw up.

"Are you insane?"

"Don't call me that!" The woman took aim, clearly not intending to miss this time. "Help her!"

Jillian drew a deep breath and gathered her scattered nerves. She sunk back into her healing trance, centering her awareness and seeping back into Emily.

The little girl had already begun to drift during the time Jillian had been gone. She didn't have the strength to overpower the armed woman or to carry Emily to the hospital herself. She could only hope she had the strength to face the shadows again, and that the woman would see reason.

She gathered her heat and battled the shadows.

♦

Emily's eyelids fluttered.

"Can you hear me, baby?" Mona cradled the bloody little girl in her arms.

Emily's blue-green eyes opened. Tears welled up in them and spilled down her round cheeks.

"Mommy?"

"Yes, baby. You're going to be okay now." She hugged the little girl to her chest.

Emily clung to her, chubby little fingers digging into her shoulders. Mona didn't mind at all. She rubbed her cheek against Emily's baby-soft one, reveling in the warmth she again felt there.

"Do you hurt anywhere?"

"No. Sleepy."

"Okay. Let's get you out of that dirty dress and find some pajamas. Then you can take a little nap." Mona kissed Emily's forehead, holding the little girl tight as she stood.

The healer lay still on the bed. Mona nudged the woman with her knee. Nothing. At least she'd healed Emily before passing out.

Mona went into the bedroom. Ms. Baare had to have something Emily could use. Mona couldn't very well carry her around in bloody clothes. People would ask questions, and questions could attract the police.

She set Emily on the bed and undressed her. A warm washcloth from the bathroom helped to remove the bloody residue from Emily's skin. Two more finished the job.

Mona threw the soiled washcloths in the corner. She didn't want any reminders of the drive-by shooting that had nearly taken Emily from her. They'd never go to a playground near a busy street again. Or any playground, for that matter.

The image of Emily falling from the swing right in front of her, bloodied and bawling, would be forever etched in her memory. Thanks to the healer, Emily was whole and healthy and still with her. Nothing could change that now.

Mona rooted through the drawers and found a white T-shirt, then slipped it over Emily's head.

"There you go, baby. You look just like a little angel." She ran her fingers through Emily's blonde curls. With Emily in her arms, she went back to the living room.

Emily twisted in her grasp. "Who that?"

"Nobody, baby. She's just taking a nap. Shall we go home now?"

Emily stared at the woman on the floor. "Down."

"No. We need to go home now."

"Down," Emily insisted.

Mona sighed. A nagging feeling in the back of her mind told her that she needed to check the woman anyway. She couldn't very well leave the healer alive to talk to the police. All the missing child posters in the post offices and supermarkets were bad enough.

She knelt down and put her hand on the still woman's lips. Nothing. Not even the faintest hint of breath. She smiled.

Emily touched the healer's face, stroking her cheek. "Night-night."

With the little girl seemingly satisfied, Mona grabbed Emily and left.

The police could make what they wanted from the bloody scene. Maybe they'd think there had been an attack. She didn't have time to waste finding the single bullet she'd fired, but the gun wasn't hers anyway. She'd bought it from some guy on the street three days ago, and who knew where he'd got it from.

"What do you think about being Canadian, honey?"

Emily had already closed her eyes. Her sure and steady breathing brought warmth to Mona's heart. No one would recognize them there; all they had to do was make it across the border.

No one stopped them when they left the hotel. Mona hummed a lullaby she remembered hearing someone sing to a baby in a movie once. Lilacs scented the air as she traveled down the sidewalk. Sunlight warmed her skin.

The rusted, silver sedan sat in the parking space alongside the park, right where she'd left it. She couldn't bear to look at the park or the swings. The park should have been a safe place, and this one was mostly vacant, which had set her at ease. There were no meddlesome people on cell phones who might call the police. Now she knew the true reason why no one played there.

A car drove by, slowly. Her heart pounded. She couldn't remember what the other one had looked like before the bullets flew. This one kept going.

Her hands shook as she buckled Emily into the stolen booster seat. Another car turned the corner and headed towards her. She ran around her car and got in, thrusting the keys into the ignition. The engine rumbled to life.

She fumbled with the radio knob, hoping to check for news reports, but it seemed to be malfunctioning on a whim. She gave up on it and headed to the nearest northbound highway. Emily's head was already resting on her shoulder, eyes closed before they got up the ramp.

Ohio had given way to Michigan before she heard Emily stirring around in the back seat.

"Waking up, baby? Do you need to go to the bathroom?"

Healer

Potty training on the run wasn't the easiest thing, but when she'd taken Emily three months ago, she'd been in underwear, so she thought she'd better keep up the effort. Besides, she didn't have money for diapers.

"I gotta go." Emily squirmed in her seat.

"We'll stop in just a minute. I need to get gas, anyway."

Mona pulled into the next gas station. After she parked the car, she unbuckled Emily.

The little girl pushed her away. "I do."

"Sure, baby, you can get out by yourself."

Emily didn't want her help in the bathroom, either. She closed the door to the stall before Mona could get in. The lock clicked.

"Let mommy in. You need help. That's a big toilet."

"No."

"Emily, really. Let me in. This isn't funny. You could get hurt."

"I do."

Mona bit her lip. This was the first time Emily had refused her help. Ever since she'd stopped crying for her other mommy and accepted Mona, she'd been very cuddly. It was almost as if she were afraid to let Mona out of her sight.

"What's gotten into you?"

Was this the "terrible twos" she'd heard so much about? As terrible as they might be, as long as she had her baby, it didn't matter. She'd love her right through two and three and every year afterwards.

The toilet flushed and the door opened. Emily walked out, her bare feet padding over the gray cement floor.

"You did that all by yourself?"

"Yep. I big girl."

It suddenly seemed so. Mona wasn't sure what to make of this new development. She liked the needy toddler better. Having someone need her made the nights warmer and the days brighter. Someone had to listen to her for a change. That felt pretty good.

"Are you hungry, honey?"

"I wash hands first."

Since when did two year olds care about washing their hands? They ate old gum from under tables if you didn't watch them.

"I'll help you. You can't reach."

She scooped Emily up and held her next to the rust-stained sink. The water dribbled out of the faucet. The soap dispenser was empty. Emily's petite face crumpled up as if she were disgusted.

"Icky!"

"You play in dirt and mud puddles and you call this icky? Silly girl."

Mona shook her head and carried the little girl into the gas station. She had to set her down to grab two sandwiches and two sodas, but kept the little girl close as she approached the counter.

"I need gas too," she told the attendant. "Give me 20 bucks worth." She ruffled Emily's curls. "We'll eat in the car."

"Don't want to go," Emily said.

Mona picked up the little girl. "That's enough, baby." She smiled at the young man and slid the cash across the counter. "Someone is grumpy today."

Emily lunged forward, grabbing the counter. "Not my mommy."

The cashier gave Mona a questioning glance as he handed her the change.

"She's two."

The cashier nodded, as if that answered everything. "It'll be a long year."

Mona held Emily tight and balanced the food and drinks in her other arm. The walk back to the car was precarious. She set the drinks on top of the car and buckled Emily back in her seat.

"What's gotten into you, baby?"

Emily sulked in her seat, not even looking at her.

Mona sighed. She put their lunch in the front seat, the drinks in the cup holders, and went to pump the gas. Another woman parked at the pump beside hers, but she didn't leave the car and kept her purse on her arm the whole time. Hopefully, there would be better opportunities for easy money in the near future, or they'd be going hungry real soon.

After squeezing out one last drop of gas, she went back around to her door only to find it locked. Emily stood on the front seat, showing off her pearl white teeth and the tiny dimple on her left cheek.

Mona swore. Apparently she couldn't take her eyes off Emily for even a minute.

"Baby, open the door."

"No."

"Emily, please." Mona looked around, but no one paid her any attention. "This isn't funny. Open the door for mommy."

"Not my mommy."

Mona laughed weakly, plastering a smile on her face. "Don't say silly things like that, baby. Open the door."

Emily crossed her arms over her chest and giggled.

"This isn't a game. Open the damn door."

"Ma'am?" the man at the pump in front of her called out. "The kid didn't touch the passenger-side door. Try that."

"Thanks." Mona flashed him her best frazzled mother smile and darted to the other side of the car before Emily caught on and continued her game. The handle creaked as Mona swung the door open. She slid inside and grabbed the troublesome little girl.

"That was very naughty, Emily. Mommy should spank you."

"Spank Mommy. Spank Mommy," Emily chanted. "Naughty Mommy."

"I'm not the naughty one, little miss. Now sit back in your seat and eat your lunch. If you stay put, I won't buckle you in until we get back on the road." Mona pulled the car away from the pump and into one of the vacant parking spaces. As she took a bite of her sandwich, she glanced in the rearview mirror.

"How on earth did you get out of your seat?"

Maybe she hadn't pushed the belt latch down all the way; the stupid thing stuck half the time. It didn't surprise her that it might have jammed and not fastened completely.

Emily nibbled at her sandwich, eating neatly for a two year old.

"All done," she announced as she held out the empty can and wrapper to Mona.

"Thank you."

Mona took the garbage and crumpled it up with her own. Making sure to keep the door open and holding one hand on it, she tossed the garbage into the can on the sidewalk.

She fastened Emily into her seat again. This time, she made sure to click it closed and double-checked it.

"I can't have you wandering around inside the car while I'm driving." She landed a kiss on the little girl's nose and then got back in her own seat.

Mona continued northward for an hour before jutting east. With all the people in Detroit, it would be easy to get lost in the crowd heading into Canada.

Emily squirmed in her seat. "Out."

"Sorry, baby. Gotta stay safe in your seat. I don't ever want you to get hurt again."

"No more heal. I free."

Mona's breath caught in her throat. "What did you say?"

"Out!" Emily yanked in the lap bar of her seat.

"No, before that." Mona eyed the girl in the rear view mirror.

Emily stared back. Her young, round face was innocent, but her eyes were anything but.

Mona's hands shook on the steering wheel. Her voice came out even shakier than her hands.

"We'll get out and play soon." She tore her gaze from the child in the backseat just in time to see the semi-truck stopped in front of her. "Damn traffic jams!" she said, stomping on the brake pedal.

A scream welled in her throat as she realized she was too close. It was too late. The front of her car crumpled under the back end of the trailer. The steering wheel slammed into her chest. The impact knocked the air from her lungs. The car came to an abrupt stop in an explosion of metal.

Mona coughed and drew a ragged breath. She glanced up to check the rearview mirror, but the windshield's shattered glass lay sprinkled over her and what remained of the front seats.

"Emily," she croaked.

The click of a seat belt being unfastened was the only indication that Emily was alive. Seconds later, the rear door opened. Mona tried to turn to look behind her, but pain kept her head pinned against the headrest.

"Emily?" Movement outside the car caught her attention. Mona's vision blurred as she tried to make out who stood outside her broken window. "Help," she breathed.

Emily came into focus. She stood safe and healthy on the gravel roadside. Breathing was so hard. Why was it so hard? Mona looked down. So much blood.

The little girl peered over the jagged glass at the bent edges of the window frame. Her words were slow and deliberate.

"Nobody can heal you now."

Plastic Teeth

by A. P. Sessler

William Burke playfully gnashed at the air with his new plastic teeth as he unwrapped a peanut butter cup. He licked the chocolate from the wrapper, then dropped it into the white plastic bag his mother held before him.

"Thank you," she said.

"Welcome," he said, noticing the odd sound of clapping canines as his jaws met. He removed the green plastic teeth just long enough to eat the candy, then placed them back in.

"Easy, Count Chomperla. If you eat too much candy, you'll get a tummy ache," Mr. Burke teased him.

"I'm not a vampire. It's a magician's cape!" William reminded his father.

"He was just joking," said his mother. "Now go play with the other children."

"Do I have to?" he whined.

"Yes. This is your Halloween party, and they're your new neighbors."

His shoulders slumped as he trudged into the center of the dark menagerie, ducking the cotton cobweb strung across the arched opening on the way.

"I hope they like him," Mrs. Burke said.

"Come on," said Mr. Burke. "A good-looking boy like that? Of course they will." He exited the dining room through the archway into the living room. Unlike William, he managed to get a face full of synthetic web.

"All right!" His booming voice filled the first floor of their two-story home as he peeled the offending substance from his face. "Does everyone have a pair of plastic fangs?"

The assorted characters gathered there proudly flashed their plastic teeth.

"Good," he said, then whispered to his wife, "Did you get all the trash?"

"Right here," she whispered back as she raised the bag full of teeth wrappers.

"The kids love them, don't they?"

The children growled at one another like little monsters, baring fierce fangs and wicked grins, squealing and laughing.

"I guess Carlo the Great would be pleased that his old gimmicks are still being used," he said.

"How did you even find them in that mess?" she asked.

"It wasn't too hard. For an eccentric old man, he wasn't that bad at organizing things. On one side of the basement, there was the magic show stuff: top hats, magic closets, trick saws and knives, and a trapdoor stage; on the other side, there were the gags: electric hand-buzzers, fake poo and vomit, whoopee cushions, and of course, plastic vampire teeth."

"And let's not forget the section in the back."

He laughed.

"I'm serious," she said. "I don't like having those kind of books in our house."

"Babe, if we were that superstitious, we wouldn't be celebrating Halloween."

"In any case, I still think we should sell it all online. I bet we could make a killing."

"Off of stuff like plastic teeth? They're probably a dime a dozen."

"The kids seem to be getting some enjoyment out of them."

"Yeah. Carlo was a great entertainer."

Plastic Teeth

"And a decent realtor," she said, leaning in to give him a quick kiss.

She felt a tug on her shirttail, followed by a tinkling bell. She looked down to find Dudley, the family poodle, standing on his hind feet. He was wearing orange and black foil bows on several strands of his hair, and a belled collar about his neck.

"No, Dudley, I haven't forgotten about you," she said to the anxious-eyed dog.

When she leaned down to pet him, she noticed William, quietly sitting on the couch by himself, apart from all the chattering children.

"Here, Dudley. Let's go play with Billy," she said, leading the dog to William. "Billy, Dudley was bored, so I thought I would bring him over to you."

"Hi, Dudley," said William, baring his green vampire teeth.

Dudley bared his own teeth and growled.

William returned the growl, sending Dudley scampering up the stairs into the master bedroom.

"Billy! Why did you do that?"

"He did it first."

"Never mind. Stay here and try to talk to someone," she said, looking up the stairs.

"I'm sorry," he said as he stood up. "I'll get Dudley and bring him back down."

"Okay, but don't show him those teeth. They scare him."

He ran up the stairs and disappeared into the bedroom.

The grandfather clock chimed eight.

Mr. Burke approached the stereo system and paused the Spooky Sound Effects CD. The room quieted.

"It's time!" he announced. "Earlier this evening, we had you all place your votes for best costume in our ballot box, so if we could have our own mad magician William come forward to help count the votes …"

"He went to fetch Dudley," Mrs. Burke informed him.

"Just a moment, everyone," said Mr. Burke.

They waited a minute, but William didn't come back down.

"Billy?" Mr. Burke called.

Still nothing.

A plump boy in pumpkin costume approached. "Mrs. Burke?"

"Yes, honey?" she asked.

"When do we eat?"

"The pizza will be here soon, right after we announce our winners."

"Okay," he said, waddling away.

"Yes, everyone. Pizza will be arriving soon, so hold your horses and wands and broomsticks and whatever else you have. And speaking of magic wands, I'll soon pull William the Great out of our magic wardrobe," Mr. Burke said, then unpaused the CD.

A witch's ghastly laughter filled the room, followed by moaning spooks and the sound of dragging chains.

William's parents walked up the stairs, down the hall and into their unlit room. From outside, they saw him staring out the bay window, his back hunched. The bright moonlight poured into the room, stretching his shadow across the floor like a piece of black putty.

"Billy? It's time for the costume contest," said Mr. Burke.

William remained silent.

"Did you find Dudley?" asked Mrs. Burke.

The boy flinched, straightened, and half-turned his head to catch her voice. Light from the hallway sparkled in his left eye.

"Did you hear your father? It's time for the contest," she said.

William turned away, hunching his back again.

As she approached, she heard his mouth in motion, chewing or sucking some curious delight.

She saw bits of foil lying at his feet, glinting in the moonlight.

"Your father and I told you not to eat all your candy. You should save it—"

On second glance, Mrs. Burke could see the orange and black bits of foil on the floor were not candy wrappers as she had assumed. They were clearly untied bows.

"Dudley?" she called, glancing about the room.

She listened for a whimper or a bark, but only heard William's soft laughter.

"What is it, Billy?" she asked.

He turned his head, and she saw something dangling between his teeth. His mouth was dripping a dark substance that couldn't be chocolate. The thing in in his mouth fell with a jingle, quickly muted by the thick carpet.

It was Dudley's collar. She looked at the reflection of the bay window. In it, she saw Dudley's lifeless body, marble-white, lying limply over William's hands. A large, bloody stain covered Dudley's neck.

Mrs. Burke slapped her hand over her mouth to silence the scream.

Someone's hand took hold of her shoulder. She jumped, turning to find Mr. Burke. He pulled her to his side, then shoved her away, towards the door.

"Leave me and Billy alone," he said.

"I'm not going anywhere without you," she replied.

"You have to help the others outside. We can't let them see Billy like this."

A soft voice spoke from behind them. "Don't worry about us."

Mr. and Mrs. Burke turned to see their young guests silhouetted in the bedroom door.

"No, children. It's time for you to leave. Billy isn't himself," said Mrs. Burke.

"Neither are we," a child replied, followed by the others' impish laughter.

A sea of green, glowing teeth appeared on the dark figures as their closed mouths opened into fiendish smiles.

"We're so hungry," they said. "We can't wait any longer."

William's parents froze, paralyzed with fear as the silhouetted crowd and their glowing mouths filled the room. Tiny, cold hands grabbed at their sides and limbs, while plastic teeth, now stronger than bone, began to tear into their flesh.

Hauntings

by Charles Ebert

By the time Edward found his old shackles and chains, the storm was almost over. He hurried to the third floor lavatory, with the hardware gathered up in his arms. Carefully, so they wouldn't clank before he was ready, he arranged the chains on the tile floor.

Edward could hear the new occupant of the house showering in the second-floor lavatory below. The man was loudly singing an aria from Don Giovanni, and Edward had to admit that the occupant had a pleasant baritone—not professional quality, but any amateur operatic company would have prized him.

The realization gave Edward pause. *There is good in everyone*, he thought. *Maybe I should give the occupant another chance.*

No, insisted another part of his mind. Edward knew he must think of himself now. The house belonged to him. His father had designed and built it, Edward had lived in it all his life, and his mother had been an occupant for more than 50 years. Memories chained him to this place.

Edward remembered racing along the length of the porch that stretched across the front of the house, and his father jumping out of the French doors of the study to scoop him up and whirl him through the air. Edward had ridden the banister down the central staircase and slid across the highly polished wood floors in the great hall.

Now, he wandered through three floors of empty halls and closed-off rooms, every sight touching off some memory.

To remain in this world, he had to stay interested in it. The house helped, but he also needed stimulation and someone to notice and appreciate him, because the memories faded a little every day. Every day of indifference brought the Light closer.

Edward reined in his thoughts. The storm was abating; the wind slowed and no longer drove the rain clattering into the windows. Soon, the opportunity would be lost.

He paced across the lavatory floor, dragging the chains. They rattled especially loudly when he drew them over the small clamshell sink. He uttered a credible moan as he clanked over the tile. Practicing in advance, while the occupant was away, had been a good idea.

Any time now, Edward expected to hear screams, slamming doors, and footsteps running down the walk outside, then he would be rid of this occupant forever.

"I take it you're the ghost."

The voice came from behind him. Edward stopped in mid-stride and turned around. There, leaning against the doorjamb, was the occupant, with his arms crossed and a towel wrapped around his waist.

He was a middle-aged man, about 45, Edward thought. Thirty years older than Edward had been when he became a ghost. The occupant was a lot better looking: not as thin and pale, and he had a strong chin, whereas Edward's was pointed.

"Yes, I am," said Edward.

"And all this," the man waved his hand at the tangle of chains on the floor, "is supposed to scare me."

"Does it?" Edward asked in a hopeful tone, which he immediately knew was a mistake.

"Worse," sniffed the occupant. "It insults me, all this Victorian cliché and claptrap. It may have worked for Dickens, but today, it could only be used to frighten a tot, and a very young one at that. Anyone old enough to have followed the adventures of Scooby-Doo with any assiduity at all would simply laugh. Which is what I'm doing."

Edward noticed, however, that the occupant wasn't laughing.

Instead, the man turned and marched away, leaving Edward to pick up his chains and return to the attic.

♦

"He's right, you know," said Edward's friend Freddie. Freddie was an agreeably chubby little ghost who, after 75 years of independence from the need for sustenance, still snacked incessantly. Even now, as they sat together on the roof of the charming Tudor cottage that Freddie haunted, he was working on a joint of lamb, offering Edward advice between mouthfuls.

"These days, you can't get away with using the chains and all that. They're too familiar with our traditions."

"What am I to do?" said Edward.

"Why do you want to get rid of him, anyway? I thought you liked people."

"Not this one. I can't get any interesting reactions out of him at all."

"Did you steal his socks?" asked Freddie, thoughtfully.

"Yes."

"Rearrange the top of his dresser?"

"Every night."

Freddie furrowed his brow and set the joint of lamb down on the roof tiles. "That is troubling."

"Can you help me?"

"I think we should talk to Old Silas."

"Oh, no. I don't want to bother him," said Edward, shrinking back from the idea.

"Why not?"

"He doesn't like ghosts," Edward said. *Which is strange*, he thought, *because Silas is a ghost.*

"Silas doesn't like anything. But if you want to scare somebody, he's your spirit. Nobody's lived on that farm for decades."

"Can't you come up with something, Freddie?"

Freddie thought it over for a minute and said, "I can give you some modern ideas, but keep in mind, I'm hardly an expert. And I'll warn you …"

"Yes?" said Edward, noticing the dark look in Freddie's eye.

"Some of them are pretty gruesome."

◆

Over the next week, Edward tried Freddie's schemes. He avoided the really gross ones at first, because he simply wasn't that kind of ghost. Sending his blood-soaked head floating down the staircase and calling out for Katherine or Victoria or somebody didn't come naturally to him, and he doubted if he could pull it off with conviction.

Edward tried throwing dishes like a poltergeist, but the occupant's china was made out of some light, unbreakable material that merely clattered on the kitchen tile. In the morning, the occupant rinsed it off and ate breakfast.

Normally, Edward was not a spiteful soul, but he couldn't contain himself. He appeared in the dining room as the occupant ate his eggs and bacon and said, "Your china is deplorably ugly."

The occupant cast him a dark look. "Mind your own business." But then the man looked down at the plate, caressing the edge with his thumb and forefinger.

Edward walked away pointedly.

Becoming invisible and rushing past the occupant to create an intensely cold draft didn't work either. The man just went up to his room and took a hunter green sweater out of the closet.

Edward sat on the dresser, watching the occupant pull on the garment. Edward had to admit that it was a very nice sweater, but the dark green washed out the occupant's already pale face.

Hauntings

As sometimes happens, the occupant sensed that Edward was in the room, even though he was invisible. The man pulled at the bottom of the sweater and then drew the collar tightly around his throat.

"I'm not going out in it," he said, "I'm just going to wear it around the house until you're done flitting about."

♦

It was time to try some of Freddie's more sinister suggestions. The next night, Edward appeared in the occupant's bedroom. The man lay in his bed, still awake, no doubt thinking repulsive thoughts. Edward leaned over and whispered what Freddie had told him to say, word for word.

The occupant sat bolt upright, and for a minute, Edward thought he had finally succeeded.

Instead, the occupant turned to Edward and said sharply, "I don't have a wife, nor do I have a dog. And I certainly do not possess a chainsaw. In future, please get your facts straight. Good night, sir." And with that, he rolled over and went to sleep.

Making the walls bleed, which Freddie had assured him was "can't miss," didn't work either. The occupant simply glanced up from his book as the gore came oozing out of the plaster in the study.

"Seen it," was all he said before returning to his reading. He covered up the title of the book before Edward could see it.

This was bad. Freddie's suggestions were almost completely exhausted. In fact, the only one left was the floating head thing, and Edward was far from comfortable with it.

Still, with the Light becoming more enticing every day, there was nothing left but to try.

♦

The next day, after setting things up, Edward sat on one of the eaves, enjoying the last rays of the sun and watching as the neighborhood kids played soccer on the lawn across the street. Edward enjoyed this world, so full of sunshine, noise, and well … life.

One of the kids kicked the ball, which bounced off another kid's head and rolled into the street. The second child ran after it. He looked both ways before running into the street, which was why he didn't see that the ball had stopped right at the feet of Edward's occupant, who was walking home. When the boy finally realized what had happened, he stopped in the middle of the street.

"Ball, Mister?" he squeaked.

There was a long pause. Edward made sure he was invisible and floated down to street level. He could see the evil thoughts parading across the occupant's face. The man even started to bend over in order to confiscate the ball, but some stray good thought must have crept in, and this initial nasty impulse was suppressed.

Instead, the occupant kicked the ball back across the street. Of course, it went off the side of his foot and wound up rolling under a car. The man turned his back on the kids and walked toward the house, but he was brought up sharply by the whispered words, "Kicks like a girl."

The occupant stood, shoulders hunched forward, hands clenching and unclenching into fists. After a seemingly endless moment of this, he shook his head and stormed up the walk to the front door.

With a last look at the kids, Edward flew toward the house and veered around the occupant, entering through the wall. He got inside just in time to see the occupant unlock the door and enter.

Edward flew to the upper hallway, and made the final preparations. First of all, he made his head visible. Then, he put blood around his neck and smeared some on his face.

The occupant entered the front hall and Edward started walking down the stairs.

"Katherine," he wailed, giving his voice a nice echo.

"Oh, for God's sake," said the occupant, pinching the bridge of his nose.

"Katherine," repeated Edward, drawing out the syllables a little more.

"I can see that you're walking, you know. Your head's bobbing up and down like a cat toy."

Edward stopped. *Oh, dear*, he thought. He had meant to float down the staircase, but in the excitement he'd forgotten.

"Well, now you've broken character. Hardly professional."

Edward cleared his throat, feeling awkward. He floated down the stairs.

"Victoria," he cried, raising his voice an octave.

"Make up your mind, man. Is it Katherine or Victoria?"

Edward winced at the lapse, and then poured his frustration into a really loud, drawn out wail. When he got to the bottom of the stairs, he found himself looking up at the occupant, who was about a head taller.

"Wouldn't scare a puppy," said the man, walking away.

Edward made himself invisible and wiped the blood off his face. With a heavy sigh, he floated through the roof and sat on his favorite eave, watching the now deserted moonlit streets of the neighborhood.

Across the way, he could see Freddie's Tudor, a cheerful little house. Even now, he could imagine Freddie doing all the normal things that a ghost does: stealing one sock from the laundry, hiding a child's favorite toy, or making the house creak in the early hours of the morning.

Most occupants delighted in that sort of thing. While not threatening, it gave them a glimpse into the other world, a dash of mystery. It was something to talk about around the dinner table with their friends, a service, really. One that Edward's present occupant didn't appreciate.

It was enough to drive Edward to despair, and more than ever, he was thinking about the Light.

He looked over his left shoulder, where the Light always seemed to be. It sparkled, but not irresistibly. Not yet. Edward had never had a desire to see what was beyond it before, but the thought was burrowing in his mind that if he couldn't successfully scare off one lone occupant on this side, maybe he didn't belong here anymore.

At that point, Freddie floated by. He lightly set down, digging into a bag of chocolates.

"Saw you up here. Things not going well, I take it?"

Edward outlined the events of the previous week.

"I warned you; I'm no expert."

"I'm not blaming you, Freddie. I probably just didn't do it right."

Freddie nodded. "Don't blame yourself, either. Serious haunting is a knack; not everybody has it."

Edward looked over his left shoulder. "I guess not."

His friend whacked him in the shoulder. "Hey, don't despair. Your man is an old enough buzzard. If you wait 20 years or so, he'll be going to the Light."

"And what am I to do in the meantime?"

Freddie shrugged. "I think it's time to talk to Silas."

This time, Edward had to agree. They started off to find him.

Silas was one of those driven ghosts that appear from time to time. A misanthropic soul, he couldn't abide any sort of occupant and could barely stomach other ghosts. He inhabited a run-down farmhouse about a mile from the city limits. It was, of course, deserted.

"What?" said Silas, after Edward and Freddie had arrived at the farm and summoned him. Silas had been old when he became a ghost. On his sharp face was a scraggily beard. He carried an axe in one hand and a bottle of liquor in the other.

Freddie started to step forward but Edward stopped him. It was Edward's problem, after all.

On shaky legs, he stepped past Freddie and stammered, "I want to get rid of an occupant." He once again recited the list of his troubles, concluding them by saying, "I expect that I've bungled the whole thing."

Silas turned his back on the pair and gazed at the farmhouse. "I had an occupant like that once. Insufferable man! He started moving furniture and putting up wallpaper. He was changing everything she had done." Edward knew better than to ask who "she" was. Driven ghosts often had terrible secrets, and judging from the way Silas was now eyeing the blade of his axe, his were worse than most.

"What did you do?" asked Freddie, who loved these kinds of stories.

"The man had a powerful fear of spiders." Silas's face broke into an unpleasant smile. "I gave him spiders."

Edward swallowed nervously. "I'm not sure what my man's attitude toward spiders is," he said.

Silas held up his axe for silence. "Listen carefully. I won't repeat this. Every occupant has his own secret fear, some deeply-buried terror that drives his every action. You must observe him and find out what it is, and then, act."

With that, the wicked old farmer melted into the breeze and flew away to whatever private Hell he inhabited.

"Well, that wasn't much help," said Freddie.

"Actually," said Edward, remembering, "I think it was."

♦

The occupant finished his shower and his aria at the same time. The last notes hung in the steamy air. Edward leaned against the doorjamb of the second floor lavatory and waited. He could see his shadow on the far wall, cast by the sparkling Light.

Pushing open the curtain, the occupant stepped out onto the tiled floor. His hand groped for a towel, and after finding it, started to dry his hair.

"You were a little out of tune during the first chorus," said Edward.

The occupant looked up, obviously startled. "I beg your pardon?"

"And your voice wavered during the higher notes."

"I don't see where it's any of your—" began the occupant, but Edward went on, seeing that the intensity of the Light had diminished.

"And as for tempo, well, what can I say? You are inconsistency itself. Perhaps you should look at the score again, with a better eye for the time signatures?"

"I was taking a shower, not singing a recital," said the occupant, taking a step back. Edward saw his shadow grow diffuse.

"Oh, you have excuses, do you? Extenuating circumstances? Just because you're wet and covered with soap, you think you are exempt from focusing on technique?"

"Stop it," said the occupant, backing away even more from Edward, whose shadow almost completely disappeared. "I know what you're doing and it won't work."

The Light brightened, its intensity rivaling the mundane electric lamp above the sink. Edward paused for a second, fearing that this plan would fail like all the others. But one look in the occupant's eyes and Edward knew encouragement. The man was afraid. Afraid of Edward! It was a new feeling. The Light dimmed again.

"I hope tomorrow, you'll do a better job. I want to see you bear down and concentrate. Stay on pitch, with a nice even tempo throughout."

"Or what?" said the occupant, defiantly.

"Or I'll come back and give you my notes, again. And I'll keep doing it until you get it right. Then we'll discuss your taste in china, clothes, and reading material, and after that, we'll address the proper way to kick a ball."

The man blanched and pressed himself against the wall.

"Stop picking on me!" he shouted. He held the towel in front of him as if it were a barrier and made a break for the door.

"And nobody uses the word 'assiduity' in everyday conversation," yelled Edward as the man ran down the hall.

Noticing that the Light was completely gone, Edward floated up to his favorite eave and watched as the occupant shot out of the front door, still holding the towel, and ran down the street.

Freddie joined him and said, "I suppose congratulations are in order."

"Thank you, Freddie," said Edward. "You know, he runs like a girl."

Freddie agreed.

Clinical Trial

by Daniel Devine

I followed the signs along the tree-lined driveway to the visitors' parking lot and pulled into one of the open spots. I beep-beeped my car alarm on, feeling a bit silly as I surveyed the expensive sports cars parked around me.

The cobblestone path leading from my car to the entrance passed through a small rest area featuring wrought iron benches and well-manicured flowerbeds. I paused for a moment to fight off a coughing spasm and made my way along the path. The silvery lobby doors resisted my first tug but swung open smoothly once I overcame their weight.

Just inside was a small sitting area, where black leather couches faced a huge flat-panel screen. A young, blonde receptionist—twenty-something and stunningly beautiful—sat behind a mahogany desk on the other side of the room.

"Hello. Welcome to Algernon Pharmaceuticals," she greeted me brightly. "What can we help you with today?"

"My name is Jack Hunter." My voice came out as a barely intelligible rasp. I had to clear my throat and start again. "Jack Hunter. I have a 12:30 with Dr. Enechono. I'm a bit early."

"No problem at all, Mr. Hunter," she said warmly, already typing on her keyboard. "Dr. Enechono always likes to get an early start on things." She pointed to a binder on the edge of her desk. "Please sign in and take a seat in the waiting area."

I smiled my thanks and sat down to see what was headlining on the news. The receptionist was right about Dr. Enechono, because he was there before the station came back from commercial.

"Mr. Hunter?"

The doctor was a short, dark, slightly swarthy man in a knee-length white lab coat. His stare was somewhat intense, but I found his appearance and manner somehow comforting. All in all, he seemed appropriately doctorly.

"Yes. Thank you for seeing me on short notice," I said, extending my hand.

The doctor touched my flesh just long enough that I could consider it a handshake and turned to begin striding down a hall to our left.

"Nonsense, I am glad you are interested in participating," he said, as I jogged to catch up. "I think you will be most beneficial to the study."

The corridor ended in an electronically-locked door that the doctor opened by waving a photo ID from his pocket. On the other side, the décor was much more spartan: spotless white walls under clean fluorescent lighting. Dr. Enechono led me to the first door on our right, which turned out to be his office.

He sat behind his desk and I took one of the two chairs facing it. His desktop was covered in paperwork, but it was neatly organized into straight rows. Without hesitation, he selected a manila folder from the center of the desk and handed it over to me. I opened it up and whistled.

"Sure is a lot of verbiage in here about absolving you of any liability for injury, suffering, or fatality. Is that typical for this type of agreement?"

If the doctor had anything resembling a sense of humor, he didn't choose to show it.

"Please understand, Mr. Hunter, this is a very serious undertaking. A stage-two clinical trial involves an untested medicine with poorly understood side effects. If you are uncomfortable with this, then I urge you to reconsider your involvement."

"Just joking, Doc." I assured him. "I mean, what's it going to do, kill me? I've only got a few years as it is."

Enechono's expression softened and he shook his head. "Before you can sign, we must review these documents thoroughly and ensure that you fully understand the commitment you are making," he insisted. "For example, page 12 contains a unique set of stipulations that I require for this research."

"Err, page 12, you said?" I fumbled with the paperwork. "Ah, the part about being required to reside in the Algernon clinic for the extent of the trial? It does seem a bit extreme …"

"Understand," replied the doctor, "that I need to keep you under constant surveillance. I want to minimize any risks by being able to deal with them the instant they are detected."

"Actually, that's not a problem. I have no family in the area and I've been on disability since last year, so I'm not working."

Dr. Enechono smiled. "You realize this means not leaving the clinic at all during that period? Our clinic will not be serving as your hotel room; you won't be allowed to leave for a day trip and come back later, or anything of that nature."

I shrugged. "Like I said, I don't really have any place I've got to be."

Enechono's dark eyes stared into mine for a moment before he apparently came to a conclusion and gave a great sigh.

"Very well, Mr. Hunter, but let us go over this page by page, as the rules dictate. Page number one …"

♦

A couple of weeks later, I arrived in the Algernon Pharmaceuticals parking lot once more, this time by taxi. I propped up my suitcase on one of the benches and sat, taking a moment to relish what would likely be the last fresh air that I would encounter for a while. There was a nice, cool breeze, but after a second, it shifted, blowing the scent of the flower blossoms toward me. The pollen made me cough, and I was forced to rise and drag my luggage towards the building, eyes streaming tears and lungs gasping for air.

I expected to check in with the pretty receptionist, but instead, orderlies in lab coats were waiting on the lawn outside. My suitcase was taken and placed on a dolly. A sandy-haired man took my license, checked it against his paperwork, and handed me a "Participant" badge. A scrawny kid in glasses then grabbed me by an elbow and took me inside. His nametag read "Matthew."

I was led into the main part of the building through the same security door as before. My guide didn't bother to pause at Dr. Enechono's office, but I noticed that his desk was unoccupied.

"It's not much further, Mr. Hunter," Matthew said. "The entry to the clinic is just at the end of the hall."

I glanced left and right as we walked, seeing smooth black tabletops covered with beakers, hot plates, and Petri dishes. The rooms clearly made up some sort of laboratory space. I was surprised when the hallway ended in a staircase leading down.

"Your clinic is in the basement?" I asked.

Matthew nodded. "Our main business is still drug research, of course. The clinic was added on later when we expanded into in-house trials."

The staircase terminated in another security door, which Matthew opened with his badge.

We entered what clearly served as the clinic's recreational room, and it looked as though my fears about being shoved into some unfurnished room in the basement were unfounded. The walls, ceiling, and lighting were just as clean and white here as in the waiting room above, and the TV was an equally expensive hi-def flat screen.

A grandmotherly black woman in a floral-printed blouse was sprawled upon one reclined chair, snoring loudly. A young boy and a stern-looking man sat on the couch besides her, watching the tube. All three were bald, just like me.

A waist-high counter topped by a glass barrier divided us from a nurses' station, where three women sat on rolling chairs, chatting. Matthew deposited me in front of them.

"It was good to meet you, Mr. Hunter," he said. "The girls will get you settled in."

A nurse with curly red hair cleared her throat to get my attention. The glass had small holes at mouth level so I could hear her. There was also a slot for exchanging paperwork.

"Name and ID, please," she said. The other nurses behind her paused their conversation and smiled at me.

"Jack Hunter." I reached for my wallet, but she pointed at the participant badge that the man on the lawn had given me. I passed it through the slot.

The redhead slid the badge through a swiper attached to her keyboard. The computer beeped, and she took a folder handed to her by the Asian nurse, made some notes on a piece of paper, and handed it to the third nurse, who put it into a rack on the wall.

"Please keep this on you at all times, even when you're sleeping," the redhead said, returning the badge.

I studiously attached it to my lapel.

"Your room has already been prepared. If you like, Anna can take you now." She nodded toward the little blonde nurse. "Otherwise, feel free to relax in the lounge and get to know the other participants."

"Uh, shouldn't I take some medicine or something?"

"You'll be given a baseline physical later this evening and the doctor will prescribe your medicine then. We won't dispense any until tomorrow morning, so that everyone is on the same schedule."

"Oh, okay." I said. "I think I'll mingle a bit in the lounge before checking out my room."

"Very good. Just call us if you need us." She swiveled in her chair and resumed her conversation with the other girls.

I plopped myself down on the easy chair opposite the still-snorting grandma.

"Hi there! My name is Jack."

The boy tried to shush me, but the man ignored him.

"Riley. This is Andy, and the sleeping lady is Dee."

I looked around the large rec room. "Anyone else here?"

Riley shrugged. "I saw one other guy come in and go straight to his room."

I fell silent, but Riley kept up the conversation.

"So what are you in for?" he asked. "I've got prostate. Pretty bad."

I grunted. "Lung cancer. May have a few years, may not."

Riley sized me up. "Heavy smoker?"

"Quit in the '70s. Wasn't soon enough, I guess."

I learned that Andy had lymphoma and Dee had some type of brain tumor. Over the next hour, another four people showed up, which left us with a grand total of eight. I had been expecting more for some reason.

Along with the guy in his room, whose name turned out to be Ernesto, there were two more women and two more men. We made some quick introductions.

The commotion woke Dee up, so I got to meet her conscious self. She seemed like a sweet lady. One or two of the newcomers tried to engage Andy in conversation, but he responded only reluctantly.

By then, Matthew and Joe, a big orderly with a square jaw who'd been manning a clipboard when I checked in, began appearing periodically to take us away for our physicals.

Eventually, Joe called my name. He led me past the nurses' station to an exam room just like every other room where I'd gotten a physical in my decades of life, right down to the Norman Rockwell print.

Dr. Enechono was standing against the counter when I entered. The knot of the tie above his lab coat was red today instead of blue.

Clinical Trial

"Mr. Hunter, a pleasure to see you. I hope you're settling in smoothly." He motioned absently towards a baby-blue hospital gown lying across one of the chairs. "Please change and step onto the scale."

Joe exited the room, closing the door softly behind me. I changed quickly into the gown, as instructed.

"Very good," said Enechono. "Onto the scale, please."

The doctor wrote down my height and weight, then made some tut-tutting noises before instructing me to lie on the table.

He proceeded to prod my arms, legs, and chest with his warm, lotioned hands. He moved his shockingly cold stethoscope around my chest and asked me to breathe deeply. The deep breaths prompted a few small coughing spasms.

Enechono pulled some sheets from my folder. "Do you know what these are?"

I knew them quite well. "MRIs of the tumors in my lungs."

He nodded gravely. "I can't tell from a manual examination, but I expect they've gotten worse since then."

So did I, which was why I had signed up for the study in the first place. Anything to counter the prevailing sense of creeping doom.

"That's nothing to worry about in the short term," he continued in a reassuring tone. "The cancer is not progressing any more rapidly than before, but it isn't slowing down, either.

"Because of this, I am going to put you on a higher dose of the experimental medicine than some of the others. Your cancer appears more resistant to treatment, having never shown signs of remission. You may experience more severe side effects."

"No problem," I told him. "Hit it with everything you've got."

"Very well. I will proceed with what I think is the safest dose," he replied. "I want to take a baseline chest X-ray. The X-ray is less accurate than the MRI, but your most problematic tumors are large enough to see clearly, so it will give us an up-to-date record for evaluating the trial."

He waved a sheet at me.

"If your cancer has grown since these shots were taken and the drug improves it back to these levels, we don't want to end up thinking it had no effect."

He opened the door and took one step out.

"Good luck," he said. "I am pulling for you. And for all of the patients, of course."

There was a strange, passionate gleam in his eye as he said it, and I found myself further enthused. Here was a guy who really seemed to live to combat cancer.

I reached out and shook his hand. "Thank you again, Doctor, for giving me this opportunity."

He returned the handshake, looking a bit awkward in the face of my gratitude. Joe arrived and took me down the hall and around the corner to a waiting area.

Only Tom—a liver-spotted old man—was sitting there. Presumably, everybody was having some type of additional testing done. I attempted to strike up a conversation, but he was intently reading an article from a fishing magazine and only grunted antisocially at me before shuffling away into one of the rooms lining the opposite wall.

I was perusing the yellowing magazines on the coffee table when a young brunette in green scrubs came and led me across the hall.

The tech's name was Molly; she was polite and quick about her business. I was seated in an examination chair and heavy lead shielding was placed over everything except my chest.

By the time I was unstrapped from the chair, dinner was served. She hit a buzzer, and Matt arrived to shepherd me to the dining area.

Food was set up along one wall, warming over alcohol burners. Little round tables, each with six seats, filled the room. Just two would have been enough to seat our entire study.

Riley, Dee, and Bob—a heavy old guy who walked with a cane—

were the only current occupants. I grabbed some chicken and spaghetti and dropped myself in next to Dee.

They were talking about the death of bookstores and how youngsters poking at their smartphones didn't understand the value of a hardcover bestseller. I joined in the grumbling for a bit.

Eventually, Dee bid everyone good night and swatted at a wall intercom to ask for a nurse. When Anna eventually appeared, I took the opportunity to tag along to bed.

Dee and I wished each other good night and went to inspect our quarters.

Our rooms were near the dining area. Mine was about three times the length of the twin bed and twice as wide. My suitcase was open on the floor of the wardrobe, and someone had hung up my shirts and pants. I decided it wasn't worth putting up the decorations that I had brought, took off my shoes, and got into bed.

♦

The next day was hardly worth mentioning—breakfast was dry toast and unflavored oatmeal, then we all sat in the lounge as the nurses came around and gave us our doses of medication, which was a reddish liquid in a little plastic cup. It didn't taste too bad, which made me worry that mine might be a placebo.

About half the people, including Dee, said they felt sick and asked the nurses to take them back to their rooms, but I felt no different, despite my supposedly heavy dose.

I sat around watching reruns all day and beat Riley and Sheila at checkers a couple of times before letting Andy beat me on purpose.

Dinner was pretty much unspeakable, and we spent the meal discussing why it was so bad. Afterward, I decided to go straight back to my room to read a paperback.

"See you tomorrow," said Riley as we parted. His eyes drifted off along the corridor. "I hope Dee's okay."

"Her?" I laughed. "She probably just decided it'd be easier to sleep the day away in her room than on the couch."

"You're probably right," he told me with a half-hearted smile.

♦

The next morning, Riley was waiting for me in the hall outside the dining room, obviously agitated.

"What's up?" I asked.

He pulled me close along the corridor wall. "Dee's gone!" he said sharply.

"What, she left?"

"No, they took her out. I think I was the only one who saw!"

"Saw what?" I placed a hand on his shoulder, trying to calm him. "Start from the beginning. It sometimes takes this old man a minute to catch on."

"I couldn't sleep. I never can, so I was awake in the lounge before breakfast. Dee must have buzzed the nurses, because the redhead put down her crossword puzzle and went off down the hall. A few minutes later, she's shouting over the intercom to the others, loud enough for me to hear from where I'm sitting.

"I asked what was going on, but they kept telling me everything was fine and I should try going back to sleep. I pretended to play along but hung out in the hall outside my room."

His eyes were staring beyond me into something in his memory and he shuddered.

"I just saw her for a second as Joe wheeled her out, but you couldn't miss it, Jack. There was a growth bulging out of the side of her head the size of a basketball. Even from that distance, I could see it!"

"Okay! Okay!" I tried to digest his story. "Her tumor must have taken a turn for the worse overnight. We're all here because we're very sick, and these things do happen."

"A turn for the worse? Did you hear me? The thing was enormous, and there was no sign of it yesterday! Something isn't right."

"Well …" I hesitated. It did sound dramatic, but I had only Riley's word to go on. "It may be that growth of that nature isn't unheard of with brain cancer. What did the nurses say?"

He snorted. "They said that Dee will no longer be participating in the study because of an unforeseen issue that is not believed to be related to the medication."

"See?" I replied.

His brows furrowed in frustration. "Did you expect they would tell me that they just realized the medicine they gave us is liquid death?"

"I'm sure the doctor will let us know if he discovers anything disturbing about the experimental drugs." I said. "Dr. Enechono was very clear on the risks; he wasn't trying to mislead anyone."

"They say just what their lawyers tell them to." Riley marched off.

They made an announcement that Dee had left, after breakfast but before our next round of medication. They almost made it sound like an unrelated event, as if she had forgotten about a birthday party she needed to attend.

Tom and Erica asked some questions but no one demanded out. We all drank our medicine, even Riley. We always had the right to get up and walk out if we wanted to.

Paranoia continued to creep through my thoughts, though, as one by one, people left to lie down in their rooms, complaining of discomfort. The nurses said often it took participants' bodies a couple of days to "get used to" a new medicine. The doctor was monitoring things closely, of course.

Eventually, it was just me and Riley. He glowered at me.

"Still think I'm crazy?"

"I never did," I told him. "There are clearly some disturbing things here, but I feel fine, and I've decided to give the doctor the benefit of the doubt."

"So as long as only other people get sick, everything is just fine?"

"No, but what the nurses said could be true, and if people don't get better, I expect they'll stop the study."

"After having done what to us?"

I folded my arms. "Leave, then."

"I can't."

"Why not?"

"I need a home run or I'm already dead." He looked toward Andy. "But some of these other folks probably have a few more years."

♦

Bob and Ernesto were removed that night, due to "unexpected side effects."

Dr. Enechono himself was in the lounge the next morning, saying he was going to perform his first round of follow-up testing today to see if the drug was having any effect, and if not, he was going to cancel the trial. He encouraged everyone to wait at least that long before leaving.

Erica and Sheila asked to leave immediately, but the rest of us decided to hang around. The nurses pulled Enechono into their station and argued with him while Joe escorted Erica and Sheila out in wheelchairs.

Enechono and the nurses fell silent. The three women must have cowed him. He made another announcement.

"Everyone, I am afraid we must meet quickly with Algernon's management and discuss the best way to handle the remainder of the trial. If you feel any further discomfort, please do not hesitate to use the intercom system. The line will be monitored and someone will be sent to assist you."

Clinical Trial

They all practically ran off down the hall and disappeared.

"What kind of ham-handed idiots have we gotten involved with?" Tom muttered. "I'll be suing for malpractice."

He took out his phone and made a show of trying to speed dial his lawyer, but there was no reception in the basement.

We continued to bicker for an hour, at which point Tom was fed up.

"That's it!" he declared. "It's clear they're running around with their heads chopped off. I was going to let them do one last test on me, but at this point, I think I trust my family physician more."

He rose and marched toward the clinic door, only to find it locked.

"What the hell?" he shouted. He pointed to where Riley was standing. "Rye, get them on the buzzer. Tell them I expect someone down here to let me out now!"

Riley slapped the intercom button and we waited for a response. He tried again, then began slapping it over and over.

"Give it up," I told him after a minute.

"What's going on?" asked Andy. He had been lying quietly on the couch during all of this, so I had forgotten him. He was sweating now and looking a little bloated.

"Looks like we'll be going home today," I told him. "We're just trying to get ahold of the doctor."

"Good," he said weakly. "Let him know I'm not feeling all that well."

Tom was fuming. "This is ridiculous! I'm going to find a way out of here."

He started going door to door, calling for help. Riley followed him out of the lounge, and I heard them calling out, along with the occasional clatter that sounded like a tray of medical equipment being knocked over.

I stayed at Andy's side, and over the next hour, watched his entire body swell like an overcooked hotdog. Tom and Riley returned, cursing. They tried banging on the doors and walls. I think they had succumbed to panic.

"Riley!"

He spun towards me, furious. "You should have listened to me!"

"We all should have listened to you!" I snapped. "And you should have listened to yourself!"

That gave him pause.

"Come, sit beside Andy. He doesn't have long."

My words hit him like a crowbar, knocking all the emotion from his face. He and Tom came and knelt, and we spent the next two hours whispering soft assurances to the boy and generally failing to make him feel comfortable.

The size he'd swollen to by the end was horrific. Fortunately, he drifted off in a confused stupor and didn't come back.

"I'm going to kill these bastards!" Riley growled, and I could see he meant it.

We raged for a while, smashing expensive machines and hurling chairs through the nurses' station window, but we failed to find any keys or buttons in there to release the door.

All the activity left me panting for breath, and I slumped into a chair

◆

A tremendous thump startled me awake. I saw Tom lying on the ground in front of me. Blood stained his lips and chin and colored the carpet red in a congealing pool around his head.

I cried out and turned away and found myself looking at the team of SWAT officers who had just burst through the door.

"Oh, God!" one of them said. His commander hushed him.

A medic rushed to my side, and I felt him taking my pulse.

"Are you alright, sir?"

I took stock a moment before answering. Actually, other than a crick in my neck, I felt fine.

"I seem to be okay," I told him. "But the others, the side effects …" At a loss, I gestured at Tom's body. "All the doctors and nurses seemed to have deserted us, but there was a middle-aged guy named Riley. See if you can find him …"

"You're safe now," the medic assured me.

A moment later, I heard a cry, and some officers escorted Riley into the room, looking red-eyed and confused but otherwise none the worse for wear.

"There are two more fatalities," one of the men reported. "Middle-aged women. They had been locked one of the back rooms. They … I can't really describe it."

Erica and Sheila, I realized. Joe hadn't let them leave after all.

Riley and I were rushed to a real hospital in separate ambulances. The medic, Anthony, rode with me.

"Thank you for saving us," I said. "But why the hell did you have to be called in? I know the drug trial went bad, but why would they abandon us in there?"

Anthony shook his head. "Apparently, this Dr. Enechono guy was completely off his rocker. Did you know that he was actually Algernon?"

"What do you mean?"

"He was the founder and sole owner of the company—a big, successful oncology firm—and bankrolled this study himself. The thing that got us knocking down your door was an anonymous call from one of the people working in the building.

"When things started going south quickly, we figure Enechono refused to shut it down, and nobody had the authority to tell him to stop. Most of the nurses and techs walked off the job."

"But it was obvious the drug wasn't working. Why keep the trial going?"

"To observe. When we raided the building, Enechono was still in his office, watching you on closed circuit and taking notes."

I shuddered.

"But that's not the crazy part. The really insane thing is the drug itself. I don't know how much you know about cancer ..."

"I didn't go to med school, but it's pretty clear that the drug is dangerous," I replied.

"The captain had me take a quick look at the personal journal Enechono was holding, since he figured I'd be able to understand it best. From his notes, it's clear that drug wasn't designed to stop cancer at all; it was designed to send it full throttle."

"Full throttle?" That didn't make sense. "So he wanted to kill all of us?"

Andy shrugged. "I can't say, but from what I read in his diary, I think he was trying to help."

I thought back to my brief interactions with Enechono. That seemed to ring true.

"Then why?"

"He had this weird belief that cancer wasn't a bad thing, but rather that it was a beneficial process in humans that had gone wrong over time and no longer functioned properly, like your appendix. That we ought to be trying to fix the cancer rather than killing it."

"Huh?"

"Think about it," he said. "Cancer cells multiply without stopping and seem be capable of living forever. He thought it was some ancient bodily system to regenerate and repair any harm that might befall us." He gave a laugh. "Crazy as a loon, but imagine if it were true."

◆

It's been a nearly ten years since all that madness, but Riley and I still mention it often. Amazingly, both of us are still alive. He's a really good-hearted guy and has become my closest friend. We go and put flowers on all of the other participants' graves every year.

My lungs have cleared up, and Riley seems surprisingly healthy. Neither of us have brought it up yet, but I can't help noticing that our gray hairs are turning darker.

Maybe we'll keep pretending that we don't notice we're both getting younger for a while, but I have a feeling we aren't going to be able to hide it much longer.

Her Father's Eyes

by Simon Kewin

Caitlin had her father's eyes. She kept them in a jar on the mantelpiece. Most people preferred a clock up there, or maybe a nice vase. Something to wedge bills behind. Caitlin liked the eyes better.

You're not really going out like that are you? You're dressed like a whore! What will people think?

The voice was angry and heavy with disappointment. It was a particular skill of her father's.

He wasn't actually talking, of course. After all, only his eyes remained. His eyes, a portion of his cerebral cortex, and the two optic nerves connecting them. No, the voice was in Caitlin's head. The voice was a part of her that he had stamped into her mind over the course of her childhood.

For many years she'd believed his words. She had to trust something when she grew up. She needed a yardstick to measure the world against. Her father had given her a poor one, but for years, she'd assumed he was right. She was worthless. Everything he did to her was her fault. When she went out she was simultaneously too ugly for others to look at and so provocatively dressed that she was inviting trouble.

She studied herself in the mirror, touching up her mascara and threading her best silver jewelry through her ears and eyebrows.

Hussy! Painted Jezebel!

It had taken her a long time to untangle the knots in her mind. The eyes were a part of the process. As an adult, she'd tried many things to make sense of her life: therapy, religion, hedonism, poetry. In the

133

end, necromancy had saved her.

Her father had told her she'd fallen in with the wrong crowd. Fortunately, the wrong crowd turned out to be just what she needed. By the time her father died, still ranting and seething at everyone, she knew enough of the forbidden arts to act. To operate.

Like a painting, the eyes followed her around the room as she got herself ready to go out. Unlike a painting, it was no illusion. Caitlin had been very careful with the eyes. Each one sat in a plastic hemisphere with the optic muscles attached. They could turn, they could focus, and they could watch. The fragment of his brain could record and understand. What it couldn't do was speak or act.

She knew he was in there. Every full moon, she had to renew the rites. As she reworked the incantations, she always caught a glimpse of him: a ball of seething rage, bound to the fragments of his body. Once, she had been small and weak. Now it was the other way around.

Finally ready, she crossed the room to stand in front of the mantelpiece.

"I'll probably bring someone back," she said to him, "if anyone takes my fancy. A guy, a girl, whatever." She liked to imagine he'd learned how to lip read. He was certainly clever enough.

Once, she'd taken great delight in doing every single thing he'd disapproved of when he was alive. A list of things to do after he died, like a bucket list in reverse. She was over that now. Now she did what made her happy, not what made him unhappy. That was a victory in itself. Still, if she could achieve both, it was a win-win.

She gave him a twirl. Her dress didn't leave a lot to the imagination. It made her feel good.

Whore! Slut! Look what you made me do!

The voice in her head would always be there, but she'd learned not to listen. It was the buzzing of an annoying fly, or a familiar pain in her joints that she had stopped noticing.

She stepped forward to stare directly into the eyes that had scowled away so much of her childhood. Sometimes she still caught that look in them, the cold fury resurfacing. It seemed to be there now. Perhaps she was just imagining it. Or remembering it. It couldn't hurt her anymore.

She smiled and blew him a kiss. "Don't wait up now, will you?" She switched off the lights and closed the door, venturing into the evening city that was ready and waiting for her.

From the mantelpiece, two eyes scanned the darkness, unblinking, unsleeping, and unable to do anything but watch and remember.

Swamplands

by Sierra July

Mud clogs my nostrils as I sink deeper and deeper into the bog. Sputtering, I manage to regain my footing, planting my squeaky sneakers on a slippery log hiding beneath several layers of mud. Frogs chirp in the distance like thousands of heartbeats performing a symphony. Fireflies drift by, lazy lanterns perfectly complementing the stars.

Instead of the night noises, the words that started this venture resonate within me.

"Listen here, Patricia." My dad slurred his words through pain. "I need you to journey across the swamp to get our winter supplies. The Council only leaves the jackets, frozen meat, and medicine out for 48 hours, and I can't get there with this busted leg."

My dad pointed to his leg, still harnessed in a sling. The only flesh visible was his swollen red foot, which he was lucky to still have after the gator took a chunk out of his calf.

They say blood smells like pennies, but it's so much more potent than that. Even with a thousand pennies stuffed in my mouth, the smell and taste couldn't have clung to my mind for as long as they did when the water of the swamp ran red with my dad in its center.

Dad sighed and rubbed my head with his sweaty palm. "I know it's a lot to ask, but our survival depends on you, Pat."

I flounder about in the mud again as I lose my footing for the umpteenth time. I curse my clumsy feet and get my head above the hot, sticky mess again. The mud slurps around me, hungry as quicksand, but I ignore the way it attempts to suck my shoes off and keep moving. I don't have any time to waste.

Most girls my age—on the outskirts of childhood, a hop and a skip from being a Miss instead of a Missy—would still be at home, attempting to cull and polish their cooking and homemaking skills, but in the absence of a son, I'm my father's only hope at surviving the winter.

Quagmire, a region of nothing but swampland in a country known for its green oases bearing life and air, can only be called a godforsaken hellhole. The Council comes in on their helicopters and drops food and winter supplies down a two-day's journey away from all residential areas of Quagmire so they don't feel guilty about a few starving dogs—and that's all we are to them, no one needs to tell me. Only in winter do we receive charity; all other times of the year, we may as well be invisible, an uncharted territory to overlook on the maps.

Night presses in on me like a beast with a thick coat, but whether the animal is tame or out to snap me between its jaws is anyone's guess.

A depressed willow tree is sagging toward me. I make use of its branches and steady myself so I can walk along my log of a balance beam.

Shadows play with my eyes. At first glance, they look like other travelers; on second glance, they become phantoms, hiding out under mud and in trees, waiting to snag me. The few stumps and dirt mounds in the water ahead seem to form the heads of drowned victims. I imagine the phantoms turning, trying to catch sight of an unsuspecting visitor so they can use a leg or arm to drag themselves free from the bog with their root hands.

But wait …

One of them is moving about; I'm not imagining it. A head-like shape swivels this way and that, then all the way around with the ease and precision of an owl. It can't be human, and yet …

Swamplands

It's a mere four feet or so from me now, and I still can't make out any distinguishing features, only that it somehow still resembles a stump. Three feet: it's climbing from the mud, pulling against the liquid's suction. Two feet: it's not a stump, more like an elongated log, coming free from the bog. One foot: it stands before me, in the center of a moonbeam, and it's all I can do not to run and scream and pull out my hair.

It is not human, but it is alive, all the same.

What stands before me isn't a stump or elongated log, but a humanoid abomination. It has a face made of wood, rigid and unchanging, and the expression it wears is one of shock or anguish, a permanent roar of pain. From its head falls clumps of what looks like hair, or more like an angry sea of moss, gray and hopelessly tangled.

"Hel ... hello," I stammer. A part of me feels like I'm talking to an inanimate object, a girl carrying conversations with trees.

I don't think I'm going to get a reply, but then the swamp thing nods. It understands! Somehow, someway, it comprehends English. I take this as a sign that I'm not in danger.

"Can you talk?" I ask.

The thing gives the tiniest of head shakes, a "No."

"Well, then, I guess you can't tell me who you are or what to call you." I pause, thinking up a solution. "How about you come with me? I'll try to learn more about you on the way to my destination. And, so we can be more familiar, my name is Patricia. I go by Pat. If it's alright, can I call you Marsh?" I chose an ambiguous name for a swamp creature, a nickname for Marsha or Marshall, since I can't tell if I'm addressing a male or female.

Marsh gives me a nod.

"Then let's get going. I'll have to stop to rest soon."

As dawn approaches, pink and orange lights touch the horizon, and the frog and cricket concerto ends. Marsh grows uncomfortable in the light, even as dim as it is, and freezes, becoming just like the real trees all around him.

It's alright with me, for now, anyway. After a full day's bleeding and sweating, I'm due for a quick break. There is nothing to do out here, so far from home, so I just lie on my back on the spongy ground, like grass at Marsh's feet.

♦

"Hey!"

I sit up with a start.

Damn! I'd fallen asleep, and when I had so little time, too. I can just picture the hours, minutes, and seconds that trickled away from me, falling straight into the swamp, never to surface again.

I glance up and see that Marsh is still at my side, almost more stone than tree. A jolt runs through my body as I feel eyes boring into me and remember the shout that woke me up.

I spin around and see nothing at first. Part of me expects that it's another swamp thing like Marsh, one that can inexplicably speak. But then I see a figure sloughing through mud, one that is obviously human … and male.

"From a distance, I thought you were a piece of driftwood," the boy shouts at me as he fights the elements to make his way nearer, "but then I saw a tinge of pale skin under your mud covering and knew that you were one of the living."

"Yes, well," I say hesitantly. "If you're here, I guess I'm heading in the right direction."

The boy laughs. "Yeah, that or we're both roaming 'round in circles."

"I sure hope not," I say, more seriously than I mean to. But really, the possibility of both of us failing is strong.

"Best get going if you want to get the gold," he says. "I don't mind you coming along; there's less than 16 hours left in the day."

Swamplands

I gasp. "Are you serious?" I really had slept too long. I wish Marsh had woken me. Marsh …

I glance my monster companion that's still standing stock-still. This boy isn't likely to go along with the idea that a living (or at least moving) tree-like thing isn't a foe. He'd either run screaming, as I'd been about to do initially, or try to protect me from it, as boys are always inclined to do in the swamps: fight when nothing needed fighting.

So do I leave my old traveling companion for a breathing one, one that was likely as vulnerable as I was to the elements? Any sane person would know the answer to that; "monster or human" shouldn't be that hard of a choice, but perhaps I'm not a sane one.

"My name is Dustin," the boy is saying. "And yours is?"

"Oh, it's Pat. Patricia," I clarify. "Pat for short."

Dustin smiles and chuckles. "Nice name."

I blush, more from indignation than embarrassment. If this guy thinks I'm lovestruck by his suave looks and language, he has another think coming. Being flustered and being unprepared for questioning are two totally different things.

"I don't think I should go with you," I say. The words have more vinegar than I intended, but I can't stop now. "I mean, I don't know you, and I was doing just fine on my own."

"Oh, th … that's fine, then," Dustin says. He looks more downcast than I expected. "I guess I'll get going then." He pauses, as if he needs my permission.

"Alright. Hope you find what we're both looking for."

"If I do, I'll signal you somehow. My family is just me, my mother, and little sister; we don't need a full box of supplies."

I'm taken aback by the generosity, but not stupid enough to refuse. "Thank you. That's very kind of you." And I mean it wholeheartedly.

"You're welcome, Pat." Dustin says my name like music, then turns and continues on his way.

I almost question my decision. I could have someone that would help me however he could, who I could trust and—unlike Marsh—someone I could converse with. I didn't know how thirsty I was for human speech until the second it was gone.

"Oh, well." I step up to Marsh and place my palm on its barky skin.

Marsh shudders to life, making me jump back, even though I initiated the movement. I was subconsciously afraid that Marsh would never move again, or that I imagined a strangely-shaped tree to life. But no, it seems that, just like I did, Marsh only needed a rest.

We waste no time getting moving again. My sleep-tired eyes feel better, less scratchy and more willing to observe. Daylight may not have worked magic on Marsh's appearance, but it has added whimsy to the swamp. The mud looks beautiful for the first time in my 17 years of life, gleaming like the surface of a shiny coin.

Hours later, I see movement up ahead. Marsh does, too, because it stops dead in its tracks again.

It's Dustin. We've caught up to him somehow, and miraculously, he's hugging a parcel to his chest. If I felt things were right, I would be crying tears of joy and waving my arms like a loon so that he could see me, but something nags at me like a mosquito bite. Then I realize what it is.

Dustin is not alone. Another swamp creature like Marsh is moving in on him, and it doesn't look friendly. For whatever reason, that thing wants the supplies, which is why Dustin is hugging the parcel to himself so tightly. Without them, his family and mine won't survive the winter, and I can't let that happen.

I quickly begin running down to the clearing where Dustin is standing. Before I get there, I see a shadow to my left, and I'm surprised to see Marsh, keeping pace with me. Perhaps Marsh was reluctant to be alone, or perhaps it had sensed my fear and anger, but regardless, Marsh has seen no more reason to hide under its stillness.

Swamplands

Marsh and I are separate but we make it to the clearing as one.

The other swamp thing backs away a bit—in confusion, I think—as Marsh and I come up behind Dustin. The ground here is a patchwork of spiny branches and plush moss, a welcome change from the sticky mud. I place a hand on Dustin's shoulder, and he turns around with such wide eyes that I would have thought I prodded him with a branding iron. He quickly recognizes that I'm not an enemy and nearly sighs in relief … until he sees Marsh.

"Pat, get back!" Dustin shouts. "There's another monster behind you!"

I almost feel like smiling at his dismay, but I know it won't help the situation, so I keep a straight face and slowly try to ease Dustin into comfort by edging closer to Marsh.

"It's alright, Dustin. See?" I put a hand on Marsh's side and Dustin gawks at me like I've sprouted feelers, but somehow, he manages to see there is no threat in our direction, so he turns back to the other swamp thing.

It stands there, eyeing us all with so much malice that I can't even comprehend that he and Marsh are of the same species.

"I don't know what that thing wants," says Dustin. "I just found the package and it came thundering out of the swamp."

"Let's just take the supplies and go," I say, putting my hand on the twine around the brown box in Dustin's hands.

A sound escapes the malicious swamp thing's throat … and Marsh's, a growl that seems to rumble the ground beneath my feet like an earth tremor. I look at them both, inadvertently pressing against Dustin in the process. Something has changed in Marsh's face—not its expression, but the spark in its eyes. Sadness has evaporated and something fiery has taken its place. Marsh is as angry as the other swamp thing now.

"Marsh, what is it?" I ask, cautiously. My hand is still on the package, fingers curling absently over the twine. "I don't understand what's wrong with you." The rumble continues from the swamp things, like never-ending thunder.

"Move back," Dustin whispers.

"What?"

"Get away from me for a second."

I'm confused but I do as he says, watching Dustin closely to make sure he didn't get greedy and dart away with the supplies he said he'd share. As soon as my hand leaves the parcel, the growling stops. I turn to look at Marsh again. The sadness I'd grown accustomed to seeing is back behind its eyes.

"The supplies," I say. "You don't want us to take the supplies. Neither of you." I look at the other swamp thing that has also backed down, but it still looks unsatisfied. "What could possibly be so wrong with taking something that was meant for us? You do understand that if we leave this neither of our families will survive the winter, right? We need food and medicine and—"

"Pat, look," Dustin says.

I turn and see that he has unwrapped the parcel right here. "What are you doing? The bandages in there will be ruined if they get dirty."

"There's something different about this package from last year's."

I see nothing out of the ordinary; the things I mentioned to the swamp things are nestled in their warm enclosure like birds in a nest. Then again, I didn't really see last year's package; my father got that one and put the whole thing in a head-high cabinet in the kitchen, saying that we'd just get out what we needed when we needed it.

This is my first time seeing all the contents at once. Suddenly, something catches my eye—a little vial that contains a liquid the color of what a night rain might smell like, something crystal blue, soothing, and pure.

"I got supplies for my family last year and the year before, before my pa passed away," Dustin says. He hesitates while the wind howls in my ears like a wounded animal with snow on its breath. I hope that

that's the reason I feel so cold. "But I've never seen this vial before."

"Maybe it's some new kind of medicine," I say. I know for a fact that in everywhere but Quagmire, technology is booming. Medicine works faster than it used to. Ointments heal wounds without leaving scars. Why wouldn't we receive a new type of medicine?

"But this doesn't have a label like the others." Dustin, deep in concentration, glares at the blue stuff as if it stank like a skunk. "See?" Dustin rummages through the parcel until he pulls out a bottle with red liquid. "This is marked cold medicine, and there's a bottle with green capsules that says they're for headaches."

I can't comment because I don't have a response to his suspicion. I want to explain away the oddity, but something about it rubs me the wrong way, too.

I take the small vial from Dustin's hands and Marsh gives a warning growl.

"What?" I ask, swinging around to face Marsh. Suddenly, I've grown very short on patience. "You can growl all you want, but I have no idea what you're saying. If you're upset about this stuff, you're going to have to explain why, because for all I know it's a cure for West Nile, malaria and every other disease that makes people drop like flies around here."

Marsh lifts an arm to point its bark stub of a finger at the vial, then to me, then to itself. It does it again, in case I don't understand: vial, me, swamp thing. Marsh closes its eyes hard, as if making a wish or a prayer, then puts its finger to my forehead.

I stifle a scream as a sharp pain and a flash of light hit me. I feel like vomiting, fainting, and crying all at once. Then the pain lifts and I'm in another world … no, my own world at another time.

I see a desperate young boy in the mud, finding the supplies he thinks will save his family and taking the package back to them in a hurry, before he freezes to death himself.

He gets home, warms his rump with the licking flames of a dying but thriving fire, and has a small celebration with his smiling mother, father, and little siblings. Winter grows harder and meaner, like a dog that got kicked and beaten to the brink of insanity, but the boy doesn't worry; his family has the supplies that will help them through.

One sibling falls ill, then both of them, then his mother and father. They run out of cold medicine, but the boy doesn't despair yet; there is one more vial, a vial of liquid sapphire. The boy divides the contents among his siblings, then his parents, and gives a remaining drop to himself to ward off a sore throat.

The boy thinks that the medicine is working because, yes, his throat is no longer raw, his siblings are running about and giggling again, and his mother and father are up and smiling, hugging each other as they look on at their children, thankful, so thankful.

But then the boy starts to notice something: his joints feel stiff. I feel it as if they were my own, bone and muscle becoming like nuts and bolts. His skin grows hard and he starts to wonder. The children no longer run around; they are statues in their rooms, eyes tearing up as their feet grow clubbed, weighing them to the floor. The woodiness spreads like wild fire through their small bodies and then, they are—

I pull away from Marsh's finger. I don't need to see anymore, can't stand to see anymore. I feel numb, but a small part of me realizes that I'm shaking, that tears are drenching my face, making it tender to the wind's chill. I am so, so cold.

Dustin puts an arm around me. I know it's him because of the feel of his flesh, something Marsh and his family lost so early on in their transformation. Dustin pours the blue vial's contents out onto the swamp floor and picks up the other supplies.

We head on, having obtained the supplies before our hours dwindled to none, but we still have to get home before the snow begins to fall.

I cast a glance back over my shoulder at Marsh and the other swamp thing, perhaps his father or a complete stranger. Marsh …

Swamplands

Marshall holds up a hand in farewell, and I answer him with my own wave. I wish I could say more.

Dustin leaves me and my share of the supplies at my home and heads back to his own family, kissing me gently in farewell. Dustin thinks of the butterflies fluttering in his stomach, and my dad thinks of our victory over the cold, but I can only think of those other travelers, the ones unfortunate enough to take the blue vial home.

The Deal

by Aline Carriere

I saw him from the living room window the morning Grandma took a turn for the worse. He was walking in the sun on the other side of the street toward our house, humming. The window was open to let in the warm June air. There were roses and peonies below, still in bud, wrapped in promise.

On that summer morning when I was 11, Death was coming to my house for my Grandma, and I could hear him humming. It was the only sound I heard. The birds and crickets were silent. Even the wind didn't stir.

Ma had sent me downstairs to watch for the priest. She'd called him early in the morning, when Grandma coughed up blood and her breathing got heavy.

Ma had let me into Grandma's room after her latest coughing episode. Grandma was lying in bed, the white sheet turned down at the top, speckled with little spots of red that darkened as I watched. Her white hair radiated in a circle on the pillow, reminding me of the sun.

Grandma moved the Bible from the bed, placed it on the nightstand, and patted the now-empty space beside her.

"You going to play baseball today?" she asked. "It looks like a beautiful day. I heard the birds earlier, but they've stopped now."

"Yeah, I think so, if Jeff and Pete want to play."

"I remember when I was a girl, I played baseball every day in the summer after school let out." She smiled at me, but I could tell she was seeing herself as a girl, the memory appearing in a vivid flash.

Then it left her. "Come give me a hug and run along. You shouldn't waste a day like today."

Grandma was a good hugger. She wrapped her arms around me, smelling faintly of lily of the valley, with just the right amount of pressure for the moment, and held me secure so there was just me and her in the whole world. It was one part of her that never grew old, even when she lay there in bed. Then, like a memory, it was over. I kissed her on the cheek and said goodbye.

I didn't know then that it was the last time I would see Grandma alive. I didn't even know when Ma asked me to wait for the priest. But I knew when I saw Death crossing the street toward my house.

He looked just like the pictures I had seen in books, and I figured other people must sometimes see him, too. He was a skeleton, wearing a full length black robe with a hood. The hood was down, and he carried a long sickle that he used as a walking stick.

When he got to the front of the house, I ran out to the porch.

"Get out of here!" I yelled. I was crying. I was angry, sad, afraid— all those things, but I didn't care. I yelled at Death and told him to get lost.

"Whoa, whoa, hold on," he said, putting up his skeleton hands in a pushing "stop" motion, the right hand still holding the sickle. His voice was deep and hollow, but the fact that he spoke at all startled me, and I forgot to cry or be afraid anymore. "I'm just doing my job."

I stared at Death as though staring at him would make him go away. Once I had his attention, I couldn't think what to say, but I was conscious that I was standing on the porch in front of the door to my house, where upstairs Grandma lay in her bed thinking about baseball and reading the Bible. I also knew that the priest hadn't come yet, and Death was there, talking to me.

Death broke the silence.

"You can see me. Most people who can see me run, walk the other way, or cross the street. Some of them scream. What are you going to do?"

"I don't know," I said, and meant it.

"You won't give me any trouble, will you?"

"I don't know," I repeated because I couldn't think of anything else to say. Then he put his skeleton foot on the bottom porch step.

"What are you doing?"

"I've got business to attend to," he said as he climbed the steps to the porch. When he stood in front of me, I realized he was at least seven feet tall. I couldn't stop him from going into the house.

"Does it get hot in that robe?"

Death stared down at me with the empty hollows that were his eyes, and I almost lost my nerve.

"I was wondering if maybe you'd like a glass of lemonade." I said it, not knowing if Death drank lemonade and without questioning where it would go if he did.

"I don't have time for that."

"Seems to me you're the only one with time."

Death threw his head back and laughed. He shook, and his bones rattled like a broken wooden wind chime.

"I guess I could spare a few minutes," he said.

I opened the front door and let him in. He looked up the stairs to the second floor, where Ma and Grandma were waiting for the priest.

"It's this way," I said. He followed me through the hall into the kitchen. "Have a seat."

Death leaned his sickle against the counter and sat down at the kitchen table. In silence, I brought out two glasses and got the lemonade from the refrigerator, keeping one eye on Death. By the time I put a glass of lemonade down in front of him, I was genuinely interested to see how he would manage drinking it.

He gripped the glass in his bony fingers, brought it up to his teeth and poured it where his throat should have been. The liquid disappeared.

"It must be hard being Death."

He made an "Ahh" sound and put down his empty glass. "You have no idea. I've had this job since the beginning of time."

"Have you ever not, you know, done your job?"

Death looked at me with his eye sockets. "I know where you're going with this, but no. I've always done my job. Sometimes it's hard, sometimes it's easy. Most times, it's just a job. When it's time, it's time." He pushed back his chair to stand and reached for his sickle.

"How about a cookie?" I grabbed the cookie jar from the counter and Death hesitated. "My Ma made them."

"Well, maybe just one," he said, glancing at the clock.

I sat down across from Death at the kitchen table, where I could watch the front door.

"You know that story about Death where Death calls out to a boy and the boy runs home to tell his grandfather and asks to borrow the truck so he can escape to the city?"

"Yeah, and then the grandfather finds Death and asks him why he scared the boy." Death said, with crumbs falling from his chin.

"And Death says, 'I didn't mean to scare him, but I was surprised to see him here.'" I continued, leaving Death to finish with the punchline.

"'I have an appointment with him in the city this afternoon.'" Death chuckled and shook his head.

"Yeah. Is that true? Did that happen?"

"Maybe. But it doesn't sound like me."

"What do you mean, not you?"

"I don't do this job alone; it wouldn't be possible. There are many others; that's how people die at the same time. We're all doing our job. And besides, I would never tell anyone beforehand when his time is coming. That's part of the deal."

"The deal?"

"What I like to think of as the cosmic deal." Warming to this subject, Death took another cookie.

The doorbell rang, and I saw the shadow of Father Henry through the screen door.

"Are you going to get that?" Death asked, looking at his cookie as though planning the next bite.

"I'll just be a minute," I said. I got up, my heart pounding, and ran to the front door, leaving Death eating my mother's cookies at the kitchen table.

"Father," I said breathless and opened the door. "Ma and Grandma are upstairs. Hurry." I didn't pause to see Father Henry go up the stairs, though I did notice his bewildered expression as I turned around and ran to the kitchen. When I got back, Death was still sitting there.

"Can I have some more lemonade? These cookies are really good."

I poured Death another glass of lemonade and sat down again. "You were saying something about a deal?"

"Yeah, the deal is this: you're born and live your life, and the only catch is that at some unknown point, the ride has to end. But your time, however long, is your own. I always thought it was a good deal. That's why I can do this job."

"Seems some people get a better deal than others."

"Not really. You're only thinking that because you're comparing one person to another, but the length of your life has nothing to do with other people. It's yours alone. It's not fair or unfair; it just is."

"What about the people you leave behind? It's not fair to them."

Death cleared his throat and gave me a sideways stare, the way Ma sometimes did when she knew I was thinking something I didn't have the nerve to say. "It's part of the deal."

"Where do you bring 'em? The people you take," I said, trying to change the subject.

"I take them up to the light. After that, I don't know what happens."

Death leaned over across the table so that I could see clear through to the back of his skull. "But I do hear things," he confided in a whisper. "Sometimes it's yelling, fighting and screams. Other times, it's music and songs more beautiful than anything I've ever heard on Earth." He straightened and took another gulp of his drink.

"Is that what you were humming before?"

"You know, sometimes I just can't get the tunes out of my head." Death paused and finished his lemonade. "Well, I guess I better be getting on. I've already spent too much time here."

I couldn't think of anything more to say, and my eyes welled up.

"My Grandma. Do you have to take her?"

"Now don't start with that."

"I can't help it. I love her. I'll miss her."

"I know," he said, putting a bony hand on my shoulder.

"I couldn't …?"

"No. There's nothing you can do. Nothing you can say."

I nodded, unable to speak.

"Thanks for the lemonade and cookies. I guess that priest should be about done now."

I looked at Death. His skeleton face didn't reveal anything, but I think he would have winked at me if he could. He got up and walked out of the kitchen with his sickle.

When he reached the stairs, I ran after him and grabbed his robe. He turned around.

"When it's my time, can it be you? I'd feel better if I knew it would be you who came for me and not some other Death." I felt selfish and ashamed, asking him to come for me when my time came while Grandma was upstairs with Ma and Father Henry taking her last breaths.

"Sure," he said, and held out his hand. I curled my 11-year-old hand around his skeleton fingers and we shook on it. Then he continued up the stairs while I watched.

The Deal

I went back into the kitchen and cried while I cleared the table and washed up. When I was done, I waited in the living room for Ma to come down and tell me Grandma was dead.

I looked out the window to where I'd first seen Death that morning, humming and walking toward my house. The birds had started to chirp and twitter and I thought how Grandma would have liked to hear them sing again.

About the Authors

H. C. Duncan was born in Melbourne in 1991.

Yegor Chekmarev is a student at Princeton University studying Chemical Engineering. His favorite authors include Arthur C. Clarke, Jorge Luis Borges, and Mark Z. Danielewski.

Madeline Popelka is a recent graduate of Yale University, where she studied physics and creative writing. She currently lives in Wisconsin.

Julio Toro San Martin is a Canadian author whose work has been published by *Innsmouth Free Press*, *The Lovecraft eZine*, *Static Movement*, Tigershark Publishing, Horrified Press, and Atlantean Publishing.

Sean Moreland is the editor-in-chief of *Postscripts to Darkness* (pstdarkness.com), a journal of uncanny fiction and illustrations, and his poetry and short fiction have also appeared, most recently, in *Lackington's*, *Despumation*, and *Black Treacle*. His essays have appeared in a number of journals and scholarly collections, and he co-edited the essay collections *Fear and Learning: Essays on the Pedagogy of Horror* and *Monstrous Children and Childish Monsters*, and is currently editing *The Lovecraftian Poe: Essays on Influence, Reception, Interpretation and Transformation*, which will be published in late 2015.

About the Authors

P. R. O'Leary writes and makes films so someday he won't have to work in a cubicle. In between these spurts of creativity, he enjoys running long distances and going to film festivals. You can find his work at www.PROleary.com, and you can find him inside his geodesic dome in central New Jersey.

Jean Davis lives in West Michigan. When not writing, she can be found playing in her garden, enjoying a glass of wine, or lost in a good book. Her short fiction has appeared in *Tales of The Talisman*, *The First Line*, *Allegory*, *Isotropic Fiction*, *Liquid Imagination*, and more. Follow her writing adventures at jeanddavis.blogspot.com.

A. P. Sessler, a resident of North Carolina's Outer Banks, is constantly searching for the unique elements that twist the commonplace into the weird. When he's not writing fiction, he composes music, dabbles in animation, and muses about theology and mind-hacking, all while watching too many online movies. His short stories have appeared online and in print anthologies such as *Zippered Flesh 2*, *Dandelions of Mars*, *Allusions of Innocence*, *Star Quake 2*, and *Cranial Leakage*.

Charles Ebert has been writing science fiction and fantasy on and off since high school. His novel, *The Sword of Dalmar*, is available from Amazon as a paperback and Kindle eBook. He has sold short stories to *Encounters*, *Kaleidotrope*, *Electric Spec*, and *Aoife's Kiss*. Two of his stories won honorable mentions in the Writers of the Future contest. He is a librarian in Durham, North Carolina. Find him at charlesebertwriter.wordpress.com.

Daniel Devine is the speculative fiction author of the *Cull Chronicles* and other short stories. A graduate of Cornell University, he holds degrees in Chemistry and History and makes his living by pretending he knows something about science. His newest standalone fantasy novel, *The Demonsword Saga*, will be released by Wolfsinger Publications in early 2015.

Simon Kewin is the author of over 100 published short and flash stories. He lives in England with his wife and daughters. His cyberpunk novel *The Genehunter* and his fantasy novels *Engn* and *Hedge Witch* were recently published. Find him at simonkewin.co.uk.

Sierra July is a University of Florida graduate, writer, and poet. Her fiction has appeared in *Robot and Raygun*, *T. Gene Davis's Speculative Blog*, and *Perihelion Science Fiction*, among other places, and is forthcoming in Belladonna Publishing's anthology *Strange Little Girls*. Follow her progress at talestotellinpassing.blogspot.com.

Aline Carriere lives and writes in Massachusetts. Most recently, her short fiction has appeared or is forthcoming in *Suspense Magazine*, *Microfiction Monday*, *Saturday Night Reader*, *The Literary Hatchet*, and the anthology *Elements of Horror*. She is @Jedlight on Twitter, where she enjoys connecting with fellow writers and readers, and looking at pictures of cats.

About the Editor

Steven x Davis is a speculative fiction writer and freelance editor. He founded *Acidic Fiction* in 2014 and currently serves as the editor-in-chief. In addition to publishing this anthology, he published his debut fantasy novel, *Favor*, in February 2014, and will be releasing his second book, *Abstract Nonsense: Stories, Poems, and Essays*, in mid-2015. You can find examples of his fiction and nonfiction writing at www.stevenxdavis.com. For examples of his editing, read this book again or check out all the stories available at www.acidicfiction.com.

Thank You!

Your purchase of this anthology keeps *Acidic Fiction* online and advertisement-free. To further support *Acidic Fiction*, you can make a monthly donation at www.patreon.com/acidicfiction or buy the next anthology in Fall 2015. In the meantime, keep reading all the new stories at www.acidicfiction.com every Monday and Friday!

www.ingramcontent.com/pod-product-compliance
Lightning Source LLC
Chambersburg PA
CBHW061216170626
46809CB00003B/1377